The Old Man Is Me

Best wishes!
Bruce Stagg

Library and Archives Canada Cataloguing in Publication
Title: The old man is me / Bruce Stagg.
Names: Stagg, Bruce, 1952- author.
Description: Short stories.
Identifiers: Canadiana 2020024650X | ISBN 9781989417126 (softcover)
Classification: LCC PS8587.T26 O43 2021 | DDC C813/.54—dc23

Published by Boulder Books
Portugal Cove-St. Philip's, Newfoundland and Labrador
www.boulderbooks.ca

Cover design and layout: Tanya Montini
Editor: Stephanie Porter
Copy editor: Iona Bulgin

Printed in Canada

We acknowledge the financial support of the Government of Newfoundland and Labrador
through the Department of Tourism, Culture, Industry and Innovation.

Funded by the   Financé par le
Government   gouvernement
of Canada   du Canada

The Old Man Is Me

BRUCE STAGG

BOULDER
BOOKS

For my grandchildren:
Nathan, Kaylee, Hailee, and Carter

CONTENTS

Preface

Newfoundland was a colony of Britain until 1949, when it joined the Dominion of Canada; much of its culture was uniquely preserved in tiny, isolated fishing communities scattered around its vast coastline. In this time before computer technology and cybercommunication, the culture remained steeped in British and Irish influences. Life was rudimentary, often arduous, but also romantic.

This is the place that has inspired my writing. Some stories were related to me by family and friends, others were taken from personal experiences. I have taken the liberty of combining some plots to create conflicts, to emphasize themes, or to make a particular story more appealing. I have also mixed around and combined various personality traits to embellish and to develop characters.

As is the case with all fictional writing, the author and the narrator are not the same person. That being said, *The Old Man Is Me* is a book of fiction infused with truth. For my family and friends, I make no apologies if you recognize a personal quality in a particular character or know a certain story all too well.

As I grow older, so do the stories that I have committed to memory, and I feel an obligation to communicate some of them. It is my hope that readers will learn about our heritage, experience our culture, but, more importantly, enjoy the stories.

The Secret

My early years in a small island fishing community are best described in the words of Charles Dickens: "It was the best of times, it was the worst of times ..." The best of times was spent meandering along the slippery, granite shoreline from East Point to Sheppard's Cove, teasing the tumbling waves and challenging them to wet a young boy's feet. Or leisurely exploring the landwash in search of corked bottles from distant shores that might have contained a pirate's treasure map or the last will and testament of a shipwrecked sailor. Looking for exotic fish that had been caught in a northern current and washed ashore to perish in a strange land. Climbing through the ballast sticks of Abe Hick's fishing stage attempting to catch a crafty conner on a hook baited with the eye of a tomcod that had been caught earlier, enticing a mature lobster from underneath a submerged rock by incessantly tapping its kelp-covered surface with a fish prong and, afterwards, using the same prong as a weapon to spear the tasty crustacean. Waking in the early morning to the putt-putt of small motorboats heading to the fishing ground and to the smell of fresh homemade bread toasting over the red-hot cinders of a well-stocked coal stove.

When the sun crossed the equator on its journey south to the Tropic of Capricorn, the best of times meant strapping on a pair of ice skates and criss-crossing the frozen harbour on the night of a full moon while the ocean moaned, groaned, and heaved underneath. It meant pushing a catamaran to the top of Clouter's Hill, loading it up with as many mates as it could hold, and, launching it downgrade, allowing gravity to create speeds that brought squeals of delight from its passengers. It meant hiding behind a snowbank by the roadside, waiting for one of the few cars or trucks in the place to come inching its way over the snow-packed surface, the sound of biting chains announcing its arrival. Then, it meant dashing like a lamplighter, grabbing the back bumper, and hanging on for dear life while enjoying an exhilarating ride to the far end of town or until a gravel spot brought an abrupt and sometimes painful end to the sport.

Christmastime was anything but humbug. It conjures memories of journeying into a stand of young fir trees, hacking one down with a dull axe, fastening it to the floorboards in the parlour, and waking in the morning to the smell of fresh turpentine on the icy morning air. Of the enchanting sound of fresh snow squealing underfoot as the whole family marched to the little, softly lit church for a midnight carol service. It was the best of times when Christmas mummers, in strange and elaborate disguises, arrived unannounced with a ruckus and entertained with festive antics of dance, song, and recitation.

The worst of times was watching my father board a small fishing schooner for a three-month trip to the distant shores of Labrador in search of the elusive cod, knowing that there would be little or no communication for the entire time, and dreading that he might, like so many before him, never return—claimed by the grim reaper of the deep. Hearing heated and anxious words drifting from behind a closed door when the trip was a failure and little or no money was made. Equally odious was witnessing once-able-bodied men return from the sanitarium in St. John's: broken and crippled from the effects of the terrible tuberculosis. Or being ushered aboard a hospital boat to be inflicted with rows of painful scratches along my lower back as protection against the same dreaded disease. The terrible embarrassment I felt each time I was forced to stand in front of my classmates and suffer one smack on each hand with a pebbled leather strap for each spelling word copied incorrectly. On days when my dyslexia seemed to take over, I received enough smacks to redden and swell my tiny hands and to cause tears to roll down my cheeks.

Nothing, though, was worse than the terror and anguish inflicted upon me by one of the community's most prominent citizens—Conrad Thompson, the most miserable of men.

Old Thompsie, as he was callously referred to by all children and a few of the more rebellious adults, was a self-proclaimed theologian, lay reader, superintendent of the local Sunday School, and the most solid pillar of the church. He had come to our community long before I was born, when he married a much younger Abigail Benedict, the only child of Charles Benedict, the owner of Benedict's General Store—the largest on the coast. Residents considered it an anomalous union, because Abigail was angelic in character and features, while Old Thompsie was as homely as Ebenezer Scrooge: "The cold within him froze his old features, nipped his pointed nose, shriveled his cheek, stiffened his gait, made his eyes red, his thin lips blue …" Nevertheless, it proved a valuable union for Old Thompsie because Charles Benedict died of a heart attack at a relatively young age and left Abigail, an only child, the entire estate.

One of my earliest memories of Conrad Thompson is of him delivering a fiery sermon that sent tingles down my spine. The image is as vivid now as it was on that sultry Sunday morning in August when I witnessed it. The sinews in his long, mottled neck were tight and visible as he pointed a bony finger and declared in a tone of absolute condemnation that certain lost souls among us were going straight to hell.

When we returned to our home, I asked my mother who it was he was pointing at—fearing that it might be me.

"No one in particular," she answered.

"But why was he so mad?"

"He wasn't really mad. It's just his way."

"But he was yelling, his eyes were popping, and his face was blood-red," I continued, pushing the issue.

My mother sniffed slowly and rubbed the back of her head the way she always did when she was perplexed and searching for an answer. "It's the way he makes people fearful, so they will live good Christian lives," she finally responded.

I did not understand her explanation, and it did little to ease my dread. If it were Old Thompsie's intention to instill the fear of God—or a fear of the devil, for that matter—he did neither. He succeeded only in instilling a fear of himself.

As superintendent of the Sunday School, Old Thompsie made frequent unscheduled visits to our classroom. His sombre presence unnerved not only me but the other students, and the young volunteer teacher as well. When he entered the room, we had to stop all activities and stand respectfully, and remain standing, with heads bowed in reverence, while he slowly walked up and down the rows of seats, executing an inspection. God help the boy whose hair rested on his shirt collar or the girl who had the audacity to paint her fingernails. On one occasion, he halted abruptly abreast of me and made two disgusting guttural coughs to clear his throat. I felt the terror of all the demons of the underworld descend upon me.

"Your father has been away fishing in Labrador this summer, has he not?"

I attempted to respond, but my voice failed me, and an inaudible whisper escaped my lips.

"Speak up, lad!" he snarled.

I took a deep breath, found my voice and blurted, "Yes, sir."

"And I believe he has returned?"

"Three days ago, sir."

"I didn't see him in church this morning," he stated in a tone that fell somewhere between contempt and cynicism. Then he marched along, leaving me shivering in my seat like a scolded puppy.

During a recess break in early spring, when the frost had left the gravel roads in its usual soft and muddy state, Barry Murphy and I raced from the schoolhouse directly to the store to be first in line at Benedicts' candy counter. Without giving a thought to cleaning our boots, we trotted directly to the candy counter. Barry made it to the counter ahead of me and ordered a 5-cent, chocolate ice cream cone. He was handing over his 5-cent piece when a huge hand grabbed him by the collar of his school blazer and plucked him hard from the counter on which he was leaning.

Startled, I looked for the source of the intrusion and found myself staring directly into the fiery eyes of Old Thompsie. My knees buckled. Before I knew what was happening, a second hand snagged my shirt collar and I, along with Barry, was dragged to a spot near the front door and ordered to stand on a large hemp mat.

"Look at the bloody mess you've made," he growled, jerking us roughly to face the inside floor. "Have you been taught nothing?"

I was much too petrified to offer any explanation or apology. My concern was that Barry, being more fearless and bolder than I, might blurt out something that would worsen our situation. Thankfully, he remained silent.

"Now then," Old Thompsie continued. "The two of you will clean up this mess. And, for being so thoughtless, you will not only clean up after yourselves but scrub the entire floor. Now, clean off them boots while I get the buckets and mops."

Once released, I immediately began viciously scrubbing my boots on the bristled mat. Barry tugged on my arm like an impatient child. "Run," he mouthed.

"No!" I snapped in a projected whisper, grabbing a fistful of his navy blazer. "He'll come to the school and get us."

Barry halted, and I knew by the way his eyes were darting from left to right that he was pondering my logic. Before Barry had a change of heart, Old Thompsie returned, toting two buckets with a mop handle sticking out of each, the length of which was greater than either of us boys. He demonstrated to us the proper way to work a mop—left to right, in a figure-eight motion—the way disciplined sailors swab decks.

We were marched to the rear of the store like two court-martialled soldiers. "Start here," Old Thompsie ordered, "and work your way to the front."

For more than an hour, Barry and I worked diligently while our stone-faced nemesis looked on with folded arms. If that was not bad enough, upon returning to school only our tardiness was frowned upon by our teacher. We were sternly lectured and issued detention for one whole week.

My next face-to-face encounter with Old Thompsie occurred the summer I turned 12, and it led to an episode that was, without doubt, the worst of my childhood.

At 12, I had already turned my back on boyish youth. I had sprung up like a weed in a manure patch and was growing hair in places where it hadn't grown before. I smoked tobacco on a *somewhat* regular basis and could roll a cigarette almost as good as my Uncle Jack. And I had already felt Jenny Murphy's right breast while we were skating on the harbour ice. It was a bitterly frosty February night and the moon was full. Jenny was wearing two sweaters and a down-filled parka and I a pair of double-knit mittens. Hence, it was not exactly an erotic episode, but it was one of those moments a young boy staring into the eyes of manhood does not forget.

To further my sense of maturity, I had been earning my own money by doing odd jobs and operating my own little enterprises. Three times a week I lugged drinking water from the community well and filled the water barrels of Mrs. Dora Keats and Uncle Bobby Bursey. I shovelled snow from pathways during the winter and chopped firewood in the summer. In the fall I picked gallons of blueberries and partridgeberries, which I sold to the collector to be shipped overseas. Springtime, I tilled and trenched potato gardens, collecting earthworms to sell to the city folks who came in droves to go trouting. I distributed the local *Fisherman's Advocate* to every household in the community, and I collected discarded beer bottles from the ditches along the roadway and sold them back to the wholesaler for a tidy profit.

My most lucrative enterprise, though, was the cod tongue industry. It entailed cutting the delicate hyoid apparatus from the discarded cod's head and selling the gelatinous portions door to door. These cod tongues, as they were inappropriately named, were considered a delicacy and in high demand, yielding fancy prices.

That same summer—the one I turned 12—Benedict's General Store displayed the most magnificent bicycle in its front window. It was this bicycle that led to my most dreadful encounter with Old Thompsie. It was bright red with shiny chrome fenders, curved handlebars, and whitewall tires. For hours I stood, nose against the glass window, imagining myself riding it along the roadway in front of Jenny Murphy's house. During these daydreaming sessions, I incessantly made calculations around the bicycle's hefty price tag—the equivalent of which was approximately one month's grocery bill for our entire household. After much sombre deliberation, I convinced myself that I needed this two-wheel beauty, and I devised a clever plan to pay for it. I had stashed away in an old tobacco tin an amount adequate enough to make a substantial down payment. The remainder I would pay off in monthly installments, acquired from my various work endeavours.

"I'd like to purchase the red bicycle in the front window," I proudly said to Alex Edmunds, the hardware manager at Benedict's General Store. Alex, a neighbour and a close family friend, always treated me kindly, and I felt comfortable approaching him.

"It is one beautiful looking bicycle, isn't it?" Alex commented in a non-patronizing tone. "But I think it might be a bit on the expensive side for you, my son."

"I can afford it, Alex. Honest."

Alex grinned and spoke softly. "I assume you have discussed this with your mother and father."

"No, not yet," I admitted. "But I don't need to because I have my own money. Well, not enough to pay for it all at once, but I can pay it out. You can charge me interest."

Then, I explained in detail: how much I was paid for each paper delivered, each pathway shovelled, each turn of water lugged, each can of worms collected, each bundle of firewood cut, and each dozen cod tongues extracted and sold.

"And, I can make even more money if I work longer and harder."

"You'll need a down payment."

"I have it here," I proclaimed, dumping the contents of my tobacco tin onto the shiny wooden counter.

If Alex had any reservation about my sincerity or capability, he did not show it. He dabbed the pencil tip on his tongue and made calculations on a piece of brown wrapping paper after counting the contents of the tin.

Finally, he spoke. "My jingles, my jingles." *Jingles,* Alex's word of choice, expressed the full range of emotions—everything from anger to pleasure. Only in the intonation of delivery could one derive its intended meaning and, on this occasion, it was perfectly clear that it meant endorsement.

"I'll take this to Mr. Thompson for approval," he said, carefully creasing the wrapping paper on which he had made his calculations.

My eyes popped open. *Old Thompsie!* The mention of his name sent a familiar chill down my spine and filled me with uneasiness.

Alex disappeared behind the big double-hung wooden

door that led to the inner workings of the store and Old Thompsie's office. Like one accused of a criminal offence anticipating the return of the jury, I waited, fiddling with the measuring tapes displayed on a metal rack and picking up finishing nails from the nail bin and letting them sift through my fingers. Finally, after what seemed like an eternity, Alex emerged. Old Thompsie trailed him.

"This lad here?" Old Thompsie asked.

Alex nodded and Old Thompsie marched up to the counter and sized me up.

"How old are you, lad?" he asked.

"Twelve, sir. Thirteen my birthday," I added, attempting to legitimize my request.

"Yes, that would be apparent," he mumbled, sneering.

"The boy is mature for his age," Alex added.

Old Thompsie ignored Alex's remark and proclaimed loudly, "Application rejected." Then, without explanation or elaboration, he retreated.

I saw my dream of owning the best bicycle in the place disappearing through solid wooden doors, and I felt tears well in my eyes. My disappointment got the better of me. I shouted out, in a totally unbecoming way, "Why not?"

Old Thompsie stopped suddenly and stiffened. Slowly he turned, furrowing his forehead so that his bushy eyebrows stood out like the hair on a cat's back when it is ready to attack. He spoke in a tone as definite as one proclaiming a death sentence. "Because, we don't give credit to boys!"

I found my voice for the second time and selected my words carefully in a pleading attempt to make my case. "But I can make the payments, sir. I already have the down payment. I got my paper route, I do odd jobs, and there's good money to be had cutting out cod tongues and selling them door to door."

A smirk cracked the corners of his drawn mouth and a puff of air escaped his flared nostrils. "You'll need to cut out lots of tongues to pay for that bicycle."

His belittling tone was not lost on me, and a flare of fury surged. "I'd pay for it soon enough if the tongues were half the size of yours," I blurted.

I heard Alex gasp and I saw an expression of shock flood Old Thompsie's face. *Where had the words come from?* They tumbled from my lips as if I were possessed by evil demons, and I searched for a way to pull them back.

"You brazen young bugger!" Old Thompsie snarled, raising his crooked, bony fingers like the talons of an attacking hawk as he lurched at me.

Alex stepped forward, breaking the path of my attacker and undoubtedly saving me from one diabolical chastisement. The fire in Old Thompsie's eyes told me that it was his intent to strike me.

My impulse was to run with all my might, but stubbornness prevailed. I composed myself, straightened my shoulders, and strutted toward the door. Before I was out of earshot, I heard Old Thompsie remark to Alex, "You had better speak to the boy's mother about this."

And speak to her he did. That very evening just after supper I peered through my bedroom window and spotted Alex making his way up the garden path to our house. Alex often made neighbourly calls, but never when my father was away. I knew all too well that this visit had a specific purpose. Fearful that I'd be summoned to give an explanation in front of him, I made a quick exit through the back door and sought refuge in the tall grass atop the root cellar. Lying there on the damp ground, I thought about the deceitful rats that invaded the dark cavity below me and lugged away healthy potatoes in the darkness of the night.

Alex's stay was short and, within minutes of his exiting the house, Mother appeared on the front bridge and called my name. My mother was a woman of some schooling and held in her memory many Shakespearean quotes which she referenced to validate certain behaviors. "If it were done when 'tis done, then 'twere well it be done quickly," was one she repeatedly used, and one that I had learned from her. Consequently, I did not tarry and headed straight for the house to face the inevitable.

She was sitting on the daybed by the kitchen stove when I sheepishly entered and presented myself.

"Alex was here."

"Yes, I saw him."

"I believe you have something to tell me."

I held nothing back and related the full details of my altercation with Old Thompsie, beginning with the bicycle in the store window. She listened intently, not once interrupting me. I cannot say that my mother was totally unsympathetic, but I was an inferior youth, and there was no defence for my actions.

I was guilty as charged, and retribution was warranted. My sentence was proclaimed with the calmness of one reciting the Apostles' Creed, and it was to be in the form a handwritten letter of apology—sincere and genuine. To this, I did not object, nor did I feel it unjust, but it was the subsequent condition of the punishment that mortified me. I was to personally deliver my letter of apology to Old Thompsie, and I was to do so respectfully.

The next day, heavy drizzle and dense fog settled upon the land, and my mood was as dreary as the weather. I struggled to compose my letter to the satisfaction of my patient mother. Sheet upon sheet of paper was ripped from my scribbler and thrown into the coal bucket, my frustration growing with each failed attempt. Finally, it was finished, proofread, and approved. Carefully, I transcribed my rough composition onto a sheet of fancy stationery—a Christmas gift to my mother from her cousin, Beatrice.

Sleep did not come easily that night. Repeatedly, I rehearsed the words I would use to approach Old Thompsie. As the foghorn droned mournfully outside my bedroom window, I pictured his clawlike hand poised above me, and I nervously anticipated his reaction to my admission of guilt.

"If it were done when 'tis done, then 'twere well it be done quickly," Mother said the next morning, folding the letter and putting it into a matching envelope.

I received it like a lowly tenant accepting an eviction notice, tucked it into my windbreaker pocket, and, heeding my mother's words, set off into the austerity of the day. I headed straight for the General Store by way of the main road. However, by the time I reached Baker's Brook, my nerve was waning, and waves of nausea were flooding over me. Hence, I altered course and took to the landwash. I meandered along at the low-tide mark, slowly circling each tidal pool, but showing no interest in the things that would have ordinarily intrigued me.

I do not know how long it took me to arrive at the General Store or how long I stood there watching people enter and leave. I do recall reaching into my little stash of tobacco to find my rolling papers wet and useless. My clothing too had become sodden with the heavy mist, and I rationalized not entering the store in such a drenched state. Like a rejected lover, I retreated around the landwash, only to find that the tide had risen, causing me to wet my feet rounding Hiscock's Point.

"You look like a drowned rat," Mother commented as I entered the kitchen. Then, almost as an afterthought, she asked. "Did you deliver the letter?"

"Yes."

"How did it go?"

"Good."

Luckily, a bubbling pot on the stove took her attention, and she delved no further into the details of my escapade. I made a speedy escape to my bedroom and sought safety under my down-filled quilt—handmade by my grandmother on my father's side. I felt shame for my cowardice, guilt for having lied to my mother, and anxiety for the perplexity of the situation. I knew that I had made things worse, and common sense told me that I had to devise a plan to deliver my letter of apology.

With the quilt pulled tightly over my head, my mind raced like a gramophone record on advanced speed. Finally, I remembered being told that it was common practice for Old Thompsie to return to his office in the evenings, after supper, to perform daily bookkeeping duties. I reasoned that, with the store vacant of customers and workers, there was an odd chance that an opportunity would present itself to complete the dreaded deed. I finished my supper quickly in anticipation of making my way back to the General Store to assess the situation.

"I'm heading out to play ball with the boys." I lied for the second time in the same day. I thought about my father, who was fishing on the coast of Labrador, and I remembered his words to me when he caught me in a lie when I was a little boy. "If you tell a lie, my son, you'll need to tell another to cover the first one, and another to cover that one, and you'll be known as a fibber." I was quickly realizing his observations to be true.

The sky had cleared and a late evening sun caused an eerie haze to rise from the wet earth. To avoid drawing attention to myself, I took to the railway track and approached my destination from the rear. It was the first time I had seen the back side of the General Store, and I noticed that it looked dreary—almost dilapidated, compared to the freshly painted, well-dressed front. A huge double-hung loading door drooped on its hinges and frowned forlornly. Wide gaps between the door frame and the side of the building were visible. I slithered through the tall grass like an eel in a kelp bed and tried to peek through the narrow opening. In doing so, I inadvertently rested my weight on a protruding metal bar running the width of the door. I heard a clicking sound. A spring mechanism released, and the big door swung inward. I tumbled inside, landing face down on the cold concrete floor.

I picked myself up and nervously inspected my surroundings. As my eyes adjusted to the dull light, I noticed that cardboard boxes of various shapes and sizes were stacked almost to the ceiling and ran all the way to the back wall in neat rows. A mixture of smells—fresh fruit, exotic spices, mint chocolate, tanned leather, and stale potatoes—permeated the air.

At the far end of the large room I noticed a light spilling from an open door. I focused on it. Immediately outside, Old Thompsie's well-worn tweed raglan hung limply on a freestanding coat rack. It was Old Thompsie's office; he was working inside. That realization caused my heart to race fiercely, but I quickly contrived a strategy that, if executed successfully, would resolve my predicament. It was a simple matter of carefully sneaking my letter of apology into the coat pocket and retreating without anyone ever being the wiser.

Cautiously sliding one foot ahead of the other and breathing quietly through my nostrils, I crept along the row of boxes aligned with the office door. When I reached the end of the row, I cautiously dropped to my knees, hunched forward and peered around the end box—a manoeuvre similar to the one I had executed many times while playing cowboys on the backside rocks. Old Thompsie's coat was only a few feet away, and I reached into my windbreaker pocket for the letter, with the intention of completing my mission. But something in my peripheral vision caught my attention.

In a designated niche on a back wall, hundreds of cartons of tailor-made cigarettes were stacked several tiers high. A variety of individual packages were lined along the bottom tier like sentries dutifully guarding the walls of a fortress. I delicately picked up one of the white packages, ran my fingers over the tight, cellophane wrapper, and sniffed it. The smell of tobacco caused me to crave smoke in my lungs. I pushed the package into my top shirt pocket, protruding my chest to imprint its shape the way the big boys from up the shore did when they came calling on young maidens. Jenny Murphy's face flashed before me, and I imagined myself opening the package and lighting up in front of her. The thought occurred to me that if I left the package in my pocket no one would ever be the wiser. I immediately dismissed the notion, though. Lying was bad enough, but stealing was strictly against the principles of my upbringing and was not in my nature. Thus, I proceeded to replace the package to the exact position from where I had taken it. As I did, my unsteady hand nudged an adjacent white package, toppling it over. It toppled another one and on down the line it went; the white sentries toppled the red ones and the red ones toppled the green ones.

I instinctively lunged forward with hand outstretched, intending to interrupt the chain of action. Unfortunately, my effort was more vigorous than intended, and I struck a base carton, knocking it askew. As a result, the entire stack foundered like an imploded building.

"Who goes there?" Old Thompsie's voice thundered.

A petrifying fear gripped me, and I froze, as a multitude of cartons tumbled around me. An ominous shadow appeared on the back wall, and Old Thompsie emerged from his office with the stock of an old double-barrel shotgun squeezed tightly against his shoulder. He had one eye cocked and was searching for a target. I ran for dear life, criss-crossing my path to avoid being in a direct line of fire. Without slowing my pace, I slammed into the back door from where I had entered and broke into the yard.

"Halt, or I'll shoot," Old Thompsie shouted, his voice sounding menacingly close.

To my dismay, I realized that crossing the yard would leave me wide open and within range of hot lead, so I frantically searched for a place of refuge. Then, I noticed the General Store's delivery truck parked against the side of the building. It was an old army surplus truck that Charles Benedict had purchased when the road was first put through the community. It was the same truck that Alex sometimes parked in the lane near his house after returning from a late evening delivery or if he was making an early morning one. I had not noticed it earlier, but it was now a welcome sight because I had discovered, while playing a game of hide-and-seek, that I could go undetected by even the most proficient of searchers by pulling myself into the cavity between the driveshaft and the pan. In a flash, I was underneath the vehicle and safely tucked away in a familiar hiding spot.

Old Thompsie broke through the door and peered into the fading light of the day. "Halt, or I'll shoot!" he bellowed again.

Peering above the drive shaft and through the rear wheel-well, I saw my attacker wildly swinging the gun from left to right. In frustration, he pointed the weapon straight into the air, pulled back the hammer, and squeezed the trigger. A deafening blast ripped through the dense stillness and resonated throughout the entire community. He walked around the truck, bent forward and looked underneath. Seeing nothing, he sounded a second warning in a tone of despondency. "I have the second barrel waiting."

My heart was pounding in my chest with such force that I feared my assailant would hear it. I bit my bottom lip and remained as rigid as the metal driveshaft on which I was poised. Old Thompsie waited, expecting, I suppose, that I would present myself with hands raised in surrender. Finally, with his tolerance spent, he pulled back the second hammer and again pointed the shotgun skyward and pulled the trigger. This time no blast rang out. Instead, there came a sick, muffled sound. A flash of flame and a puff of smoke exploded at the gun's breech and dispersed around the shooter's head. The gun flew from Old Thompsie's grasp onto the ground. He fell to his knees and covered his face with both hands. "Good God Almighty, I've been shot!"

I dropped from my hiding spot and ran like the wind, across the yard, through John Clarke's potato patch, and into the bushes beyond. I worked my way discreetly through the backwoods paths and arrived home without encountering a single person.

"What's wrong with you, my son?" My mother questioned me when I entered the kitchen. "You look all out of sorts."

"I feel a bit stomach sick," I responded truthfully.

"Go lie down for a spell if you're feelin' unwell."

Happily, I obeyed and headed for the stairwell. As I passed the mirror at the head of the steps, I noticed the reflection of a ghost looking back at me. No longer could I control my emotions. A flood of tears erupted from the depths of my soul. I muffled my sobs with my hand and ran quickly into my room and locked the door. I did not take to my bed, though. Instead, I took up position at the window, from where I had full view of the community.

As I had expected, everything was abuzz. People were darting here and there, doors were opening and closing, and a large group had gathered near the public wharf. Alex ran from his house, pulling on his jacket, and headed in the direction of the General Store. From the house next door, Mildred Lane rushed through her back door, bolted through the gate joining our properties, and headed straight across the garden to our house. In the time it had taken me to travel from the General Store to home, the news had made its way to Mildred's ears, and she was eager to share it.

I positioned myself above the upstairs heating grate to eavesdrop on the conversation.

"Hold ya tongue! Something shockin' is after happening!" she blurted as she barged into our kitchen.

My mother, who tolerated Mildred (the distributor of all news and much gossip) with mild politeness, calmly asked, "And what is so shocking, Mildred?"

"A thief broke into the General Store and Mr. Thompson has been shot!"

"Shot ... as in shot dead?" asked Mother.

I closed my eyes, clenched my teeth, and held my breath.

"No, but he's hurt bad ... the doctor is there now ... the Mounties are on the way ... the robber is on the loose." Mildred continued with an incoherent litany of speculation that caused my nausea to intensify and my heart to race. I retreated to my bed and pulled my quilt tightly over my head as I continued to sob. I felt as cunning as the rats that lurked in the darkness of our cellar.

I yearned for sleep to free me from my torment, but I twisted and turned, and sleep did not come. When the old Westminster wall clock in the downstairs hallway chimed at midnight, a startling thought brought me upright. *The letter! Where was the letter?*

I hopped from my bed, scurried downstairs, and frantically searched my windbreaker pockets. They were empty. I desperately tried to remember the details around the time I had reached for the letter. Did I actually retrieve it, and, if so, what had I done with it? Had it fallen at the moment when my attention became diverted? If so, it was sure to be found and my destiny sealed. On the other hand, if it fell outside, there was the possibility it could go undiscovered, or become soaked and illegible. Reluctantly, I returned to my bed and to a hellish night of torture—the first of many that summer.

The following several days were more burdensome than a boy of my age should have endured. I moped about the house waiting for someone of authority to come for me. Each time a vehicle rounded the corner near Alex's house, I peered through the disturbed dusk expecting to see a police car. Whenever I heard footsteps on the back porch, I expected to see a uniform. Mildred made regular visits to convey updates, and I listened to each word with mortified anticipation.

"It's almost too much to believe," she exclaimed, trying unsuccessfully to conceal her excitement. "If Mr. Thompson dies, it'll be the first murder in this place."

On another visit, she announced that the robber was considered extremely dangerous, and everyone was advised to lock all doors and windows. Shortly after, she reported that a special constable had been deployed from the city and an arrest was imminent.

The arrest never came. As the days passed, Mildred's

reports became routine, repetitive, and less menacing. It seemed that Old Thompsie was to survive his injuries. He had received a serious laceration to his right hand and a nasty burn to his face, but he would not lose an eye, as first suspected. Consequently, my anxiety subsided slightly, but I continued to skulk around the house and worry myself sick. At one point I strongly considered confessing my deed and suffering the consequence, but I could not muster the courage. My dear mother attributed my lackadaisical behaviour and poor appetite to the notorious "summer complaint."

When school reopened in early September, I returned with as much enthusiasm as a spawned-out lumpfish. My classmates talked relentlessly about the notorious break-in, and all presented inflated details and boasted preposterous theories about who was responsible and what had happened. I absorbed it all, taking little comfort in the fact that I alone held the absolute truth.

The return to school meant unavoidably encountering Old Thompsie, and it happened on the very first day, when the entire school population trailed to the General Store at recess time to purchase a treat. As he did each year on the first day of school, he met the students at the front door and laid down the rules to be followed while in *his* store.

"One line for boys, one line for girls ... have your money ready ... and there will be no horseplay!" he thundered.

I held my 10-cent piece tightly in my palm and buried myself deep in the queue of classmates. I tried to avoid making eye contact with him but was drawn to the burn scar on his face. It was purple and blotchy, but, surprisingly, it did not deface him. Rather, in a bizarre way, it complemented his ugliness.

On the first day of Sunday School he made his usual visit, introducing himself to the newcomers as the superintendent of studies in charge of Christian and moral learning. Then, he proceeded to perform his proverbial inspection. Whether it was pure fear on my part or simply my imagination, but I was certain that he halted abreast of me for an extended period. I reasoned that he did not speak to me because he knew that my father had not yet returned from Labrador.

As I grew older, I stopped visiting the General Store, gave up Sunday School, and attended church on special occasions only. Consequently, I saw less and less of Old Thompsie and the worst of times was no more.

In fact, I saw Mr. Conrad Thompson for the final time on the day of my high school graduation ceremony. As Sunday School superintendent and church lay reader, both he and his wife, Abigail, were given a special invitation to the graduation dinner. Both were expected to join the receiving line to shake hands with each of the 14 graduates. When it came my turn to shake hands with the man whom I feared more than any other, I reached for his scarred right hand like one reaching for the handle of a boiling pot. I had been taught by my father that a handshake should be firm and sustained to indicate self-confidence, but Old Thompsie's handshake was much more than firm. He gripped my hand and squeezed hard until it hurt. His bony fingers bit into my flesh, and I felt the same terror as I had the summer I was 12.

My graduation from high school left me in a quandary about my vocation in life. My heart drew me to the sea and fishing, but the unpredictability of the stocks and the impoverished state of the industry gave me reason to question my passion. Mother felt that I should pursue a higher education and become a clergyman, a teacher, or maybe a policeman. The idea of a higher education intrigued me but, when I thought about becoming affiliated with the church, I could think only about Old Thompsie and the hypocrisy of it all. I assumed that I could not spell well enough to become a teacher, and I knew little about policemen, other than a huge fear I had acquired the summer I was 12. After that, what else was there?

My dilemma was more or less solved when my father returned from Labrador with only enough fish to feed a dozen families for the winter. He declared that it was his last voyage—come hell or high water.

"'Tis a pauper's life, my son," he pronounced. "Don't you go at it. Do anything else, but stay away from the fishin' ... it'll tempt you and bait you. In the end, it'll leave you a poor man."

And stay away from it I did, as far as I could get. We had recently voted to become the newest province of Canada, and people from all over our island—young and old—were being drawn to the modern, mainland cities like blue-arsed flies to fresh cow manure. I too became caught up in the trend and the glamour. On a sunny autumn day, at the age of 17, I stuffed my father's abandoned seaman's bag with the few possessions I owned and boarded a coastal steamer heading for a popular central Canadian city—the name of which I could not properly pronounce.

After many days of travel, I ended up in a land as unknown to me as the Greek underworld: superhighways with screeching sirens, soaring buildings with coded security systems, moving stairways with serious faces, sprawling factories with smoking stacks, and trains that ran underground at high speeds. I was a little fish in a large tumultuous sea—a tiny cog in a large wheel that never stopped moving. I quickly discovered that many words common to my vocabulary had no application in this place and I was often asked to speak more slowly and repeat myself. I struggled to fit in, but it was like learning to walk again, which was not an easy task, because I already knew how to walk.

After much time and effort, I began to adjust to my new environment, shedding the outer coat of my identity and learning to wear one constructed of bogus fabric. At times, rudimentary jokes were made about my homeland and my people, and I denied my ancestry, remained silent, and pretended to be someone I wasn't. I worked long. I worked hard. I made money. I lost money. I found love, and I lost love. Rarely did I think about home and the life I had left behind, as I became absorbed in my new life.

As the years passed, life became routine and wearisome. I realized that roots do not fertilize in asphalt, and I thought about the place of my birth and the people who meant the most to me. At times a certain smell or a particular piece of music made me homesick. I remembered soft winds blowing off the ocean, caressing my face and singing me to sleep. I recalled the smell of salt meat boiling on a red-hot woodstove, and I could see friendly smiles radiating from sunburned faces. I thought about my mother, who was now all alone. I regretted not having gone home for my father's funeral—a decision that would haunt me for the rest of my life. I wondered about Jenny Murphy but did not have the courage to ask about her.

Then, one hot and humid day, while suffering the intricacy of an urban traffic jam, I experienced an epiphany. The smell of salt air filled my nostrils, the sound of screeching seagulls echoed in my ears, a chilly fog cooled my burning skin, and a vision of my mother loomed in my rearview mirror. It was too much to ignore. I decided to reverse my course.

My mother's voice sounded feeble when she answered the telephone. "I'm coming home, Mom," I blurted without preamble.

"That would be so nice. How long are you staying?"

"It's not a visit, Mom. I'm coming home to stay."

There was a sustained pause as the phone line cracked and hissed. "Oh, my," she mumbled. "Are you sure? Did you say that you were coming home to stay?"

"Yes, Mom. I'm coming home to stay."

I could not see, but I could hear her tears as she unsuccessfully sniffed them back.

"Your father would have been so happy," she added,

after I gave her the details of my travel plan.

As our conversation was ending, she added, "By the way, Mr. Conrad Thompson passed away last night."

Old Thompsie. I had not thought about him in a very long time. I was uncertain how to react. I felt nothing; my emotions were numb. "Really," I commented.

During my years of living away, my mother had kept me updated about the changes that were happening back home, but I was unprepared for what I saw when I arrived. The drab little community had taken on an air of vibrancy. Houses, once starved for a coat of paint, were now brightly coloured and draped in vinyl. The dusty, gravel roads had been widened and black-topped. Cars with rusty fenders and bald tires had been replaced with shiny new pickups. Benedict's General Store was adorned in neon lights, with a liquor store attached to it.

Refrigeration technology had transformed the once-disadvantaged fishery into a lucrative industry. Large modern fishing vessels landed load after load of fresh fish for processing. The once-lazy fish plant had become a beehive of activity with men and women in plastic aprons and hairnets running about like mainland factory workers. Work was in abundance for anyone who wanted it, and the pay was good. Most of my classmates had secured comfortable jobs at the plant and went to work in the morning smelling like their bulging lunch bags and returned in the evening smelling like stale urine. They seemed happy and content with their lot in life. Jenny Murphy, I learned, had pursued a higher education, was teaching school in the city, and was happily married with a family.

News of my homecoming spread through the community like a birth announcement. Within the first few days I was offered employment at the fish plant. I was flattered with the offer and thrilled that work was so readily available, but my father's words echoed in my ears. Nevertheless, I rationalized that this fishery was not the same as the one my father had been engaged in, and I began my new job exactly one week after returning home.

When I returned from my first shift, Mother was sitting at the kitchen table waiting for me.

"You look tired. How was it?"

"I enjoyed it," I admitted. "A little tiring, yes. But no stress, no long commute, and a few good laughs."

"Guess who came to visit today?" She abruptly changed the topic.

"I don't know. Mildred, I s'pose, with a bit of gossip."

"No, it was Mrs. Abigail Thompson."

"Old Thompsie's wife?" I furrowed my brow.

"Yes. And a lovely lady she is."

"What on earth did she want?"

Mother sniffed slowly and rubbed the back of her head as she handed me a sealed manila envelope. "She brought this."

"What is it?"

"I don't know. Her husband had requested that it was to be delivered to you after his death."

If a draft of wind had blown through a crack in the window, it would have toppled me over. *My God. He's dead and gone but he continues to torment me.*

I held the envelope gingerly, as if expecting it to explode, and I stared at my name inscribed across the front in impeccable penmanship. Blood drained from my face, my legs grew weak, and a cold sweat permeated my every pore. The events of that awful summer when I was 12 played out in my mind like scenes on the big screen. I saw a shiny bicycle in a store window. Dozens of cod tongues lay in a white enamel pan. Alex dabbed the tip of his pencil on his tongue. Stacks of cigarette packages fell. I was running. A double-barrel shotgun exploded, and Conrad Thompson fell to the ground.

"Go on ... open it," Mother insisted, breaking my reverie.

Slowly, I tore the corner of the envelope, inserted my index finger and ripped away the glued flap. Within lay a single sheet of glossy paper. It was rumpled and tarnished, but I instantly recognized my letter of apology. I removed it and handed it to my mother. She received it like a schoolchild reaching for a report and read silently, mouthing each word and nodding her head to punctuate each sentence. She smiled broadly and handed the letter back to me.

"Imagine. He kept it all this time."

Almost ceremoniously, I replaced the letter in the envelope from which I had taken it. I uttered not a word. Words from *Great Expectations* resounded in my head: *The secret was such an old one now, had so grown into me and become a part of myself, that I could not tear it away.*

The Culler

"Madeira ... Madeira ... Choice ... Thirds ... West Indie ..." Percy chanted the words melodiously, pausing only when another yaffle of dried salt codfish was placed on the wooden culling table in front of him. It was a routine workday for Percy Cuff, diligently grading fish into various piles according to the market for which it was most suitable. For the past two hours he had been culling a shipment belonging to Albert Keel, and Albert was scrutinizing the entire process.

The standards of culling for Newfoundland sun-cured codfish depended on the degree of perfection, in appearance and quality.

Choice or *Merchantable* fish was of superior quality: reasonably thick, smooth in texture, cleanly split, properly salted, and perfectly clean, with no blood stains or yellow casting. It was intended for the Mediterranean market and fetched the highest price for the fisherman and the merchant.

Madeira was of a slightly lesser quality and, consequently, lesser in value. It took a keen eye like Percy's to distinguish any imperfection that would change the grade of Choice to that of Madeira.

Thirds, the next grade, was worth less again. It was often over-salted or torn, making it a comparatively easy cull.

The substandard *West Indie* traded to the poor areas of the Caribbean for molasses and rum was sunburned, over-salted, poorly split, or had tears and perhaps prong holes. Per pound, it was worth less than half of the value of Choice.

Fish that was less than 12 inches long was labelled *Extra Small* and of almost no value.

Percy knew each of these grades like he knew the letters of his own name and could distinguish each in a glance. He had learned the trade from his father, also a well-known culler. Percy was licenced by the government of the time as a bonafide fish culler and was currently employed by the firm of R.T. Sparkes Company Limited as its top culler. Percy was a valued and respected employee of the firm for reasons other than being an expert culler. Excluding Levi Baker, the wharf manager, Percy was the only wharf worker who had earned a high school education. Consequently, during the off-season, he assumed other meaningful jobs and was frequently sent on fish-buying missions or assigned to inventory and tabulating duties. It had been Percy's intention to attend college to become a schoolteacher. He had met all of the entrance requirements and was securing a boarding house in the city when he learned that Belinda, his 16-year-old sweetheart, was pregnant. Out of love, not obligation, Percy cancelled his plans for a higher education and married Belinda before she began to show.

Besides being good at his job and valued by his employer, Percy was well respected by the fishermen. They trusted him to give their fish a fair and honest cull— that is not to say that he was not sometimes challenged when judgments differed.

"Choice ... Madeira ... Madeira ... Madeira ... Thirds ..." Percy continued calling the cull, feeling a gnawing ache between his shoulder blades from standing too long in one position.

Levi left his office overlooking the wharf area and approached the culling table. "That looks like good quality fish you got there, Albert."

"Not bad. It's been a good summer for making a bit of fish," Albert replied, not taking his eyes off the culling table.

Levi abruptly turned his attention to Percy. "You're wanted in the office, Percy."

"In the office? Me? What for?" Percy paused his work, puzzled.

"I don't know," Levi responded.

Percy immediately thought about the account that he and Belinda were conscientiously trying to balance. Was this why he was being summoned to the office? But why was he being singled out? All workers for the firm operated on a credit system and most were perpetually in debt. It was no easy task raising four children, and he could not see anything changing anytime soon. Belinda was again with child—due in just a few months—and Percy Junior was heading off to university in the city. He was a loyal employee of the company; hopefully, they would understand.

"As soon as I finish culling the last of Albert's fish." Percy resumed the task at hand. "Choice ... Madeira ... Choice ... Madeira ... Thirds ..."

"I wouldn't delay too long. It's the big man himself, R.T., who wants to see you," Levi interrupted. "I've already asked Crawford to finish up here."

"R.T.!" Percy choked out. "Why in the world does R.T. want to see me?"

"I have no idea." Levi smirked. "Must be something important."

Percy felt his face flush and he became anxious. He hoped that Albert did not notice. *Why is the most successful fish merchant on the entire northeast coast requesting a meeting with me?*

R.T. Sparkes ran his business from inside the walls of his office. Rarely did he come to the wharf, and never did he have personal interaction with wharf workers. Communication was always done through Levi or one of the office employees. Other than a simple greeting, Percy had only once been in the company of the man who had been his employer for his entire working life. This was on the unfortunate occasion of Timmy Lister's funeral. Timmy, a friend and co-worker of Percy's, was accidently killed on the wharf when a tub of salt being lifted from the hold of the firm's schooner broke loose, crushing him to death. Timmy's wife requested that Percy deliver the eulogy at the funeral—a task he found most difficult but felt obligated to perform. Consequently, Percy shared a reserved pew at the front of the church with R.T. Sparkes, who, as Timmy's employer, brought a message of condolence on behalf of the firm.

Percy's mind raced. It was unlikely that this meeting was about an overdrawn account—that would have been left to one of his assistants. Recently, he had heard whispers that R.T. Sparkes Company Limited was negotiating the purchase of the famous Ocean's International Exporting Company. Maybe it had something to do with this, but Percy could not possibly imagine how that would involve him.

Perplexed, the culler silently turned to Albert with a look that requested permission to abandon his duty.

"It's all right, Percy. You'd better not keep the big man waiting," Albert affirmed sympathetically, sensing Percy's uneasiness. "Crawford will give me a fair cull."

"Thank you, Albert," he answered, returning to the job at hand until his replacement arrived.

Then, like a schoolboy summoned to the principal's office, Percy rushed from the wharf and crossed the road to the company's elegant two-storey office building. When he reached the large double-glass door with the company's logo stencilled on the outside, he paused, feeling the urge for a cigarette—a habit he had beaten years ago.

He pushed open the door and stepped into the building. He quickly scooted past the general office and climbed the steps to the second floor, where Mr. Sparkes's office was located. On the landing, at the top of the stairs, he was met with another glass door, one that was tightly shut. *Was this the private door to R.T.'s office or did it open into a reception area?* He did not know. He had never been to the second floor, so he halted. *Will I knock or simply walk in?* He peered through the translucent corrugated glass but everything was distorted, like the time almost-blind Tommy Hiscock had him look through his eyeglasses.

He rapped softly. There was no response. He rapped again, a little harder. Still no answer. Frustrated, he reluctantly edged open the glass barrier and poked his head inside. He saw a small foyer with two chairs on either wall and a counter separating it from a larger space within. He stepped inside to the smell of mahogany and the tapping of a lone typewriter echoing off the wooden walls and furniture. Shirley Coombs, Mr. Sparkes's personal secretary, was sitting behind a large desk making the keys jump.

Percy inched his way into the small space, walked to the counter, and leaned on it. He grunted and coughed several times before Shirley acknowledged him. "Oh, Percy, I'm sorry. I didn't see you. Is there something I can help you with?"

"Mr. Sparkes wants to see me."

Shirley looked surprised. She methodically ran her

finger down the page of a large appointment book. "I don't see. Just one second, Percy. I'll be right back."

She promptly abandoned her typewriter and made her way down a narrow hallway, the click-clack of her high heels resonating off the bare walls. She halted before a large wooden door at the end of the corridor, tapped lightly, and entered the room, closing the door behind her. The sound of muffled voices spilled from the space within and Percy strained to hear what was being said. All of a sudden, he was struck with a horrifying thought. *What if this is some sick prank?* It would not have been the first time that someone on the wharf had suffered the embarrassment of a poorly thought-out joke. Before he could work himself into a panic, Shirley reemerged and joined him at the counter.

"Follow me, please," she requested matter-of-factly, lifting a hinged hatch to allow him inside.

Like an obedient child, Percy followed the sophisticated Shirley down the corridor. Percy's heart was racing when she swung open the large wooden door, stood back, and ushered him into a place as sacred as the hallowed halls of purgatory.

Mr. R.T. Sparkes was sitting behind a large cluttered desk, wearing a pair of half-framed reading eyeglasses that rested on the tip of his nose. R.T. was a big man—not fat, but jolly looking, with a red face. He reminded Percy of a picture of character he had once seen in a Charles Dickens book.

"You wanted to see me, sir?"

"Yes, indeed, Percy. Do come in." R.T. peered over his spectacles, showing only the whites of his eyes.

"Thank you, sir." Percy inched his way uncomfortably across the shiny hardwood floor like one creeping over thin ice.

R.T. stood up and extended his hand across the desk. "It's nice to see you, Percy."

"Likewise, sir," Percy responded, feeling the big man's grip and thinking that his comeback was rather inept.

"Have a seat." R.T. indicated a large, high-back chair with red velvet padding.

Percy looked at the chair and then down at the front of his salt-stained coveralls. "I'm not fit to sit down, sir. I've been culling all day."

"Nonsense, Percy. It's only salt. Nothing cleaner than salt. Salt is good. Good as money, they say."

Percy settled into the chair like one squatting on a cold outdoor toilet seat.

"Well, Percy, how's your family?"

"My family is good, sir. Thank you for asking."

"It's four children you have, isn't it?"

"Yes, sir. Two boys and two girls. And one on the way, due the month after next."

"Well, my congratulations to you, Percy, and to your good wife as well."

"Thank you, sir. I'll pass it along to her."

"And, your boy, the older one. I believe he finished school this spring. Did he not?"

"Percy Junior. That's correct, sir. They grow up way too fast. My wife says we don't own them; we only borrow them."

"That's a fact. And, I hear that he has top marks in his graduating class."

"Yes, sir. We are very proud of him. He's heading out to the university in the fall—wants to be a schoolteacher." Percy was surprised that R.T. Sparkes knew anything about Percy Junior's accomplishments at school.

"And you should be proud of him, Percy. Not every man can brag that his son has a university education. It comes with a hefty price tag, though. There will be big sacrifices to be made, no doubt."

"We are well aware of it, sir. But the boy is in the running for a couple of scholarships. He's worked exceptionally hard for it, so we're keeping our fingers crossed. If he's successful, it will go a long way."

"Well, sounds like he has his father's work ethic. I'm

sure he will do just fine. Now, let us drink a toast to his success and to his future."

R.T. swivelled his chair to face a large wooden cabinet. A gold-faced clock with decorative hands and roman numerals was inlaid in the upper half of the cabinet, while the bottom consisted of a set of double doors and a full-width drawer. R.T. pulled open one of the doors and removed an elegant decanter and two tulip-shaped glasses.

"Cognac from France," he announced, pouring a small amount in each glass and handing one to Percy. "Cognac is known as the finest of all spirits—distilled from grapes. Did you know that, Percy?

"No, sir, can't say that I did."

"Cheers, Percy! To your boy. May his accomplishments be huge. And to the good health of your wife and new child."

"And cheers to you, sir," Percy replied, clicking the other man's glass.

R.T. passed his nose over his glass and softly inhaled. "Ah, nice aroma." Then he swirled the liquor by gently tilting the glass forward and backward. He brought it to his lips and delicately sipped, making a slurping sound. "Pass it slowly over your palate, Percy, enjoy the texture."

Percy took the lead of his boss and sipped the fiery liquor the way he was taught to sip from the communion cup at the altar rail.

R.T. exhaled a long breath after swallowing his first sip. Then, he picked up the triangular decanter, held it up to the light of the window, examining it carefully. "What colour is this bottle, Percy?" he eventually asked.

What a strange question. Percy grew uncomfortable.

"It sure looks green to me, sir," he answered after giving the bottle a good sizing up.

"Now that's a matter of how you view it, Percy. When I turn it to the light like this, it looks blue."

Percy reached for the decanter and took it from R.T.'s hand. He held it up to the light and slowly turned it around and around, allowing the liquid inside to swish about. "Well, it does have a bluish cast to it when I turn it a certain way, but I still say it's green."

"So, it depends on the way you look at it, would you say, Percy?"

"It's in the eye of the beholder." Percy emitted a little chuckle in an attempt to ease the tension that was mounting within him.

"On that we do agree. Everything is in the eye of the beholder." R.T. took the decanter from Percy and returned it to the compartment from which he had taken it.

Then, inexplicably, R.T. produced a large flat cardboard box—from either beneath his chair or desk, Percy could not tell—and placed it on his desk. Like a child opening a birthday present, he folded back the flaps to reveal a large sun-dried codfish. "Now, Percy, what do you think of this?" He lifted the fish from the box.

Puzzled, Percy furrowed his brow and stared directly at his superior, looking for an explanation. His guts crawled. "I don't understand, Mr. Sparkes."

"There's nothing to understand, my friend. What I am holding in my hands is our livelihood—mine and yours. Now, what cull would you give it?"

Percy was now totally perplexed. *Was this a test? Was his ability as a culler being challenged?*

"You want me to cull this fish, sir?"

"Yes, Percy. How would you grade this fish?"

Percy felt obligated to play along. He reached for the fish like a priest receiving a newborn at a baptismal font, laid it on the table, and, taking much longer than he would have with any fish on the wharf, proceeded to apply his trade. "This is a Choice fish, Mr. Sparkes ... top grade," he declared, trying to sound confident.

R.T. leaned back in his chair, folded his arms, and spoke in a relaxed tone. "That's a matter of opinion, Percy. Someone else might see it differently. Maybe, Crawford, for instance, might see this fish as being Madeira."

Percy had had his cull questioned by fishermen on many occasions but never by a superior. He felt challenged, and he doubted himself. Consequently, he returned his focus to the fish laying ominously in front of him. For the second time he picked it up and gave it a thorough examination. He poked it, bent it, and smelled it. He had to be certain that his boss was not trying to trick him. After careful consideration, he was convinced that his first impression was correct.

"All due respect, sir, but I cannot in good conscience call this fish anything but Choice."

"But it is in the eye of the beholder, Percy. You said so yourself."

"I did indeed, sir. But I don't understand. Are you saying that this is not a Choice fish?"

"What I am saying, Percy, is a little prudence on your part could save the company a lot of money, secure your position, and perhaps mean an increase in your pay."

The comment almost knocked Percy off the fancy chair. "Are you asking me to be deceitful, Mr. Sparkes?"

"It's in the eye of the beholder, Percy."

"But, sir, I've always done my job in a fair-minded way. Every fisherman expects it of me and they deserve it."

"There's no doubt about it, Percy. But you also have to think about yourself, your family ... and the firm."

Son of a bitch. His feelings were bouncing off the walls. His emotions were as mixed as those of a jilted lover. He had to get away and think.

"I need some time to digest this, sir. So, if there's nothing else, I should be on my way."

"But you haven't finished your drink, Percy."

Percy did not know why, maybe it was because he did not want to insult his employer, but he uncharacteristically picked up his glass and drained it in one swallow. He felt the heat of the liquor warm his belly as it went down, and he plunked the glass down on the desk, not aggressively, but with a clank that echoed through the hard office space. "I thank you for the drink, sir," and he headed for the door.

R.T. stopped him with his voice. "Percy," he called.

Percy stopped and turned around.

"Remember, it's all in the eye of the beholder. And, Percy, I need not remind you that this conversation stays within the confines of this office."

Percy did not respond further. He hurried from the office, down the stairs, and bolted into the street. Just as he was stepping into the roadway, the 6 o'clock whistle sounded, ending the workday. He was relieved that he did not have to return to the wharf to face Crawford, Levi, and the other workers. Rain was falling in torrents and the foghorn groaned mournfully, but the distraught worker did not notice. He walked in a daze, along the roadway from his workplace to his home.

When he entered his house, he said nothing, ate little for his supper, and was short with the children. "What's wrong with you this evening, Percy? You're as broody as an old hen," Belinda commented.

Later in the evening, when the two were alone in their bedroom, he opened up. "I'm thinking about quitting my job, Belinda."

If Percy had said he was leaving her and the kids, she would not have been more shocked.

"What do you mean, quitting your job? Have you lost your senses? I thought you loved your job."

"I do love my job. Or at least, I did."

"You *did*? What happened?"

"Mr. Sparkes called me into his office today."

Belinda perched on the edge of the bed, her body language begging for more details.

"He questioned my integrity, Belinda." Then, in a remorseful tone, he related to her the entire conversation.

Belinda verbalized what Percy had thought. "Son of a bitch," she said, looking toward the bedroom door to make sure it was closed. "I would never have thought that Mr. Sparkes was that kind of a man."

"Nor me. That's what makes this so difficult to accept," Percy added, running his hand through his hair and over his forehead. "What am I to do, Belinda?"

"I don't know, but quitting your job isn't an option."

"I can always find something else."

"Something else! Stop and think for a moment, Percy!" Belinda's tone was deliberate and challenging. "What else is there, other than going in a fishing boat, and we both know what that is—an unpredictable pauper's life."

"But I have my pride, Belinda!"

"It can't be all about you, Percy. You have a family. Percy Junior is off to college in a few weeks. I have a child in my belly, and we can't make ends meet now as it is. Sometimes you have to swallow your pride—we can't feed ourselves on pride."

Percy knew his wife was being logical, but it did not make things any easier or help him see things more clearly. "I don't know, Belinda. I just don't know," he remarked. "I have to sleep on it."

That night, he barely closed his eyes. He tossed and turned and revisited the conversation with R.T., over and over, word for word. He thought about how things might have been easier for him if he had gone to college and about how he desperately wanted his son to have the opportunity he had missed. When he finally did nod off, he dreamed about his father, and how he preached honesty and demanded it from each of his children.

The next morning, he drank the third cup of tea before heading to work, and, for the first time in his life, arrived at the wharf just as the 8 o'clock whistle was sounding. Albert Keel was waiting for him, with a second shipment of fish.

"I was beginning to think you'd slept in, Percy. Figured you and Mr. Sparkes must have gotten into the juice yesterday." Albert joked as Percy approached the culling table.

Percy made light of Albert's comment with a chuckle, knowing full well that Albert was burning to know why Mr. Sparkes had called him to the office. He began to cull. "Choice ... Choice ... Madeira ... Choice ... Thirds ..."

Albert took up his usual position at the end of the table scrutinizing the whole procedure the way he always had. There was little opportunity for Percy to exercise "prudence" if he had wanted to.

However, when he was near finished, he picked up a Choice fish. "Madeira," he called in his musical tone, throwing the fish upon the Madeira pile. Albert said nothing. Maybe he was not paying close attention after all.

Shortly after the lunch break, Percy was again called to the culling table. Vince Sheppard had a shipment of fish to be culled. Vince was considered by most to be a little simple-minded because of the way he spoke in accented giggles and by his overall demeanour. He was one of the poorest fishermen in the place but perhaps the hardest worker. When he was younger, Vince had contracted tuberculosis and had spent six months recuperating in the sanitarium in the city. In spite of losing a lung, he returned to the fishing boat and struggled to provide for his family. Then, shortly afterwards, Vince was dealt another devastating setback—his wife suddenly passed away, leaving him to raise three young children.

In spite of everything, Vince forged ahead and remained jovial and good-natured. Everyone knew of his state of affairs and was sympathetic to his needs. Churches sent food hampers at Christmastime, and people directed their hand-me-downs his way.

Vince Sheppard was not Albert Keel. When his fish was offloaded and prepared for culling, he disappeared to ramble about the premises, to joke, and to carry on with some of the men.

Percy was left to be as prudent as he needed to be.

"Madeira ... Madeira ... Thirds ... Thirds ... Thirds ... West Indie ... West Indie ..."

As the last of Vince's fish was being culled, Percy felt a tickling sensation on the side of his neck, just above his shirt collar. He flicked at it with his salt-grained hand. Then, another prickle on the other side. He shrugged his shoulder, slightly turning his head. In his peripheral vision he caught a movement and snapped around to see Vince pinching a broken seagull feather between forefinger and thumb.

"Got ya!" Vince cackled.

Percy could not help from laughing. Then, as one is drawn to one's own name written on a page, his focus was drawn to a large patch on the knee of Vince's coveralls. It was loud and incongruous and poorly sewn—like a child would have done. Percy's father's face flashed before him. His expression changed, a surge of nausea flooded over him, and he felt himself grow weak. He raised his hand to halt the supply line.

"Has anyone seen Levi?" he asked.

"I'm over here," Levi answered from somewhere behind him. "What is it? What do you want?"

Percy turned to see Levi approaching. He waited until he was abreast of him before he spoke. "You need to get Crawford. I'm done here. I'm going home."

"What's wrong, your kidney stones acting up again?"

"No, I'm finished."

"What do you mean, you're finished?"

Percy straightened up and squared his shoulders. "Levi, I quit!"

Levi and Vince looked at each other in disbelief. The comment was heard by all within earshot and a murmur trickled through the crowd. Then, Percy turned away from the table, brushed the salt from his coveralls, and walked away.

Levi looked at the men in the supply line. Each man shrugged his shoulders simultaneously. He looked at Vince. "I only tickled his neck with a feather," he said, almost apologetically.

Belinda was in the kitchen sitting on the daybed when he returned home. He was expecting a confrontation, but he did not care.

"I was expecting you long before this," she said with a grin. "I got the kettle on."

"Belinda, I've quit my job."

"I'm not surprised."

"Can you understand?"

"Yes, Percy. I know you better than you think."

Percy went to her, sat beside her, and placed his hand on her round belly. "It'll be all right. I promise."

It was another restless night for Percy. He agonized over what the future held in store and what his next move should be. Percy Junior was going to college, no matter what—nothing would ever change that. If he had to go fishing, he would. He could always go away to the mainland—perhaps sail the Great Lakes. Word had it that a lot of men from the south shore were making big money on the lake boats. In his mind he replayed the events of the past two days. The whole situation seemed surreal. Deep in his gut he knew he had done the right thing.

Percy had the fire lit and the kettle boiled before daylight the next morning. When the 8 o'clock whistle sounded at the wharf, he was in his woodpile behind his house making kindling. It felt strange not to be reporting to work. He could only imagine the chatter that was happening on the wharf, all at his expense. Steady jobs were hard to come by, especially a good job like the one he held. It was unheard of for anyone to quit a good job.

He drove his sharp axe into a small spruce junk. It split easily. Glancing up he noticed a flicker of the curtain in the kitchen window of the house next door. Vera was peeping at him. Vera was a kind soul and a good neighbour, but she was a notorious gossiper. No doubt she had heard the news about Percy quitting his job and was anxious to learn the details. Percy knew that she would soon come fishing for information.

"Tell her nothing," Percy instructed Belinda as he

dropped an armful of splits in the wood-box. "Before I divulge any details to anyone around here, I have things to work out—a lot of thinking to do."

Shortly after 10 o'clock Percy was sitting at the kitchen table drinking his third cup of tea when the telephone sounded—two long rings and one short.

"That's our ring," Belinda said, running into the hallway to answer it. "Hello ... yes ... yes, he's here ... I'll tell him ... thank you very much ... goodbye."

Percy knew by his wife's polite tone that she was not speaking with Vera, as he had expected.

Belinda returned to the kitchen twisting her hands in her apron. Percy met her gaze, questioning her with his eyes. "That was Shirley Coombs. Mr. Sparkes wants to see you in his office."

"Mr. Sparkes? Are you joking?"

"May the Almighty strike me down."

"When?"

"As soon as possible."

Percy silently sipped his tea, staring intently at the tea leaves sticking to the sides of the cup. His grandmother claimed to have had an ability to read tea leaves, to gain insight into the future. He wished now to possess his grandmother's ability.

Finally, he pushed the cup away and stood up. "Get me my dress pants and white shirt, Belinda."

"What do you think it's about?"

"I don't know, my dear, but it can't get any worse."

Percy did not knock on the glass door at the head of the stairs. He pushed it open and stepped directly into the reception area. Shirley, who was waiting for him, immediately escorted him down the same hallway as she had done two days earlier. R.T.'s office door was ajar. She pushed it open, announced Percy's arrival, and ushered him inside. Percy flexed his shoulders and straightened his posture, determined not to be intimidated.

R.T. was sitting on the corner of his desk with his arms folded, looking out the window facing the wharf. "Come in Percy. Have a seat," he directed without turning around.

"I'll remain standing, sir, if you don't mind."

R.T. stood up, turned to face Percy, and spoke in a monotone. "Well, Percy, I'm told that you have quit your job. Have I been given correct information?'

"Yes, sir, that's correct," Percy answered in military fashion.

"And why did you do that, Percy?"

"I did it, sir, because my father taught me that right is right and wrong is no man's right."

R.T. grinned slightly. "You're a proud man, Percy."

"I have little else, sir—other than my family."

"I understand, Percy, and I am not surprised. I suspect our conversation the day before yesterday was the reason for your decision?"

"I'd be lying to say otherwise, sir."

"Well, Percy, I have not been totally honest with you. Allow me to explain and maybe you will see things a little differently."

"It seems to me, sir, that everyone's honesty has been questioned lately—my own included," Percy remarked, sensing a softening in the tension.

R.T. nodded in agreement while opening the liquor cabinet and removing the same fancy decanter as before, along with the same two glasses. He proceeded to pour cognac into each. Percy raised his hand and stopped him when he began filling the second glass. "Not for me, sir."

"Before you refuse, Percy, please hear me out," he asserted, continuing to fill the glass intended for Percy. "Have you heard that I have been in the process of purchasing Ocean's International Exporting Company?"

"I heard it rumoured on the wharf, sir, but I didn't know if there was any truth to it."

"Yes, the wharf has ears and eyes and sometimes knows things it shouldn't. The truth is, Percy, negotiations have been ongoing for a while, and the deal was finalized last week. R.T. Sparkes Company Limited has acquired the entire holdings of Ocean's International."

"Well, I offer you my congratulations, Mr. Sparkes, but did you call me here today to tell me this?"

"Yes, Percy, as a matter of fact, that is exactly why I have called you here today."

"I'm afraid I don't understand, sir."

"As you know, Percy, Ocean's International is a big concern. I have committed myself to oversee the firm's operations from corporate headquarters in the city."

"So you'll be moving away to live in the city?"

"Is that the talk on the wharf, too?"

"No, sir, it's an assumption on my part."

"Well, your assumption is correct, Percy. I need to have my finger on the pulse of operations—at least for a while. And, in the meantime, I need someone to manage this arm of the business, to take full control and to report only to me. Percy, I want you to be that person."

Percy slowly sank himself into the chair that he had refused earlier. Hairs raised on his neck and his head felt giddy. If he was confused before, he was now mesmerized.

"Me, sir? But, what about our conversation?"

"Percy, I know you are qualified for this position, but qualification is only a part of what I need. I need someone with integrity, someone I can trust—trust without doubt. I need someone who sees a bottle for the colour it is and is willing to defend what he sees."

The words swirled in Percy's head and he pondered them, trying to make sense of it all. Finally, he understood. "So, you were testing me?"

"Yes, Percy. I'm sorry to have put you through this, but I had to be absolutely sure. You did not disappoint me."

Percy visualized the events of the past two days. He saw Albert Keel standing at the end of the culling table. He saw himself tapping on a glass door, and Shirley Coombs tapping the keys of a typewriter. He saw R.T. Sparkes filling two glasses with cognac. He saw Belinda holding her belly and growing frustrated. He saw Vince Sheppard holding a feather and laughing. He saw Vera flicking her kitchen curtain.

R.T. broke his trance. "So, what do you say, Percy? Will you accept?"

"I have a question, sir."

"What is it, Percy?"

"What colour is that bottle?"

R.T. picked up the decanter and held it up to the light and studied it before responding. "It's green, Percy. It's green."

"Are you sure, sir, no questions asked?"

"I am sure, Percy, no questions asked."

Percy picked up the glass of cognac. "In that case, sir ... Cheers." And he sipped slowly.

Poor Norman

When I was seven years old, I broke my right leg, and I spent the entire summer lying on a makeshift bed in the kitchen with a cast plastered from the tip of my toes all the way to the top of my hip. I searched my mind for any possible deviant behaviour that might have warranted such retribution—no scavenging the landwash for exotic treasures, no climbing crabapple trees for bitter fruit, no enticing innocent tomcods onto baited hooks. Was it because I had crawled into Cecilia Maidment's henhouse and deliberately smashed her eggs, or was it because I had told Jack Ryan his nose looked like a banana? Whatever the cause, I was certain that my affliction could only be dealt to those destined for the fiery bonds of hell. Of this there was no doubt in my mind, considering that the devil himself, Norman Donelson, delivered the punishment.

It happened on the last day of the school year. I was enthusiastically running down the main road waving my report card like a surrender flag when a bicycle ridden by Norman struck me from behind and knocked me flat on the ground and ran over me. I recall the taste of gravel in my mouth, and my leg folding like rubber when I attempted to stand. I remember my older brother lifting me in his arms like a baby and carrying me home. And I will never forget the sound of the devil's hideous laughter as he remounted his rusty old bicycle and rode away.

Norman Donelson was one of the Donelson clan who lived on the outskirts of town, between the cemetery and Strawberry Marsh. His father, a notorious drunk who never worked a day in his life, feuded regularly with everyone. His mother came out of the house only to go to the hospital to have another youngster. Norman was the oldest and, without a doubt, the most brazen.

I was knocked down directly in front of Charlie Strickland's house and Charlie had witnessed the whole thing—me having drawn attention to myself with my ceremonial antics with my report card.

"The brazen bugger ran over the boy on purpose," Charlie told my mother.

An accident was one thing, but the thought of it

having been deliberate incensed my mild-mannered mother. At the first opportunity she approached Norman and questioned him about what had happened. She was expecting some sort of an explanation or perhaps a half-hearted apology. She got neither.

In a brazen display of disrespect, Norman looked straight into my mother's face and jeered: "Kiss me ass … kiss me ass." Then he jumped on his bicycle and rode away, patting his backside and laughing hideously as he had done when he struck me down.

When my leg healed and my fears of never being able to walk again were assuaged, I was soon running and jumping as I had always done. I ended up with a right foot that turned slightly inward and a petrifying fear of Norman Donelson.

On my 10th birthday my grandmother gave me a new bicycle—not just any bicycle, but the one from the glossy cover of the mail-order catalogue. With chrome fenders and moustache handlebars, it was a bicycle like no other around. My imagination knew no limit as I proudly rode it through town, holding the curved handlebars just as Uncle Robert held the steering wheel of his pickup.

One day, while practicing delicate riding manoeuvres on the street, I was suddenly surrounded by three beat-up old bicycles that appeared out of nowhere. It was Norman and two of his brothers.

"You got a new bike," Norman said, as if he were telling me something I didn't know.

"Yes."

"Where did you get it?" asked the brother with the perpetual snotty nose.

"I got it for my birthday," I answered, feeling the knot in my stomach tighten.

"Can I have a ride?" Norman asked.

I searched for an appropriate response to refuse his demands without placing myself in a confrontational position. Finally, I mumbled, "I'm not allowed."

"Oh … Mommy's boy is not allowed … Mommy won't let him," mocked the third brother in a childlike voice.

Then, like a cowboy roping a steer, Norman jumped from his bicycle, letting it plummet to the ground. He grabbed my handlebars with both hands and forcefully jerked forward, causing me to lose my balance and almost topple over.

"I don't care if you're allowed or not," he shrieked. "I want a ride, so get the fuck off."

The sight of Norman's junky bicycle lying on the ground reminded me of my badly broken leg, but I was powerless to protest. I reluctantly slipped from my mount and slowly pushed my prized birthday present toward the menacing form. "Don't be gone long," I stammered.

I held my breath hard, resisting the urge to cry as I watched Norman race his two dirty-faced siblings down the road and out of sight, whooping and hollering as they went. Like an abandoned puppy, I dejectedly sauntered to the main road and sat on the front steps of the post office. A cold wind blowing off the water chilled me, so I pulled my windbreaker collar tight around my neck and waited ... and waited. When the postmistress locked the front doors, ending the business day, I knew that Norman was not coming back and that it was time for me to go home.

As I turned the corner bringing my house into view, I noticed my mother standing on the front bridge looking out.

"I was worried about you," she declared as I approached. "Where were you?"

I attempted to respond, but the words choked in my throat, and the tears I had been holding all afternoon burst out uncontrollably.

"What's wrong?" she asked anxiously. "Where's your bicycle?"

"Norman Donelson took it." Sobs shook my voice.

"He *took* it? What do you mean?"

"I let him ride it, and he didn't come back."

"Why did you let the likes of Norman Donelson ride your new bicycle?"

"I don't know. I told him I wasn't allowed. He didn't listen ... there were three of them there," I blurted, sniffing back the tears, feeling ashamed and cowardly.

"That's all right, my son. You did nothing wrong. Everything will be okay." She put her arms around me, hugging me tightly.

Mother was waiting for my father when he arrived from work and met him in the porch. Through the closed kitchen door, I heard their voices whispering, then I heard the outside porch door slam hard. From the kitchen window I observed my father swing open the front gate and walk off with heavy strides.

"Where's Dad going?" I asked timidly when my mother re-entered the kitchen.

"Gone to get your bicycle."

The thought of my father confronting Norman— and perhaps his repulsive father as well—stirred an excitement within, and I wished to be brave like him. Visualizing how a confrontation might play out, I pressed my nose to the glass and watched and waited for my father to return. As the light of the day began to dissipate, he rounded the corner carrying my bicycle on his shoulders. Through the shadows of the evening I noticed that my shiny, new bicycle was covered in mud and dirt. When he leaned it against the front bridge, I saw that the front wheel was deformed, like the reflection of a full moon on water.

"I found it thrown in the ditch out on Strawberry Marsh," Father announced as he entered the kitchen.

"Is it damaged?" Mother inquired.

Father looked straight at me and chose his words carefully. "It's all full of muck. Has a few scrapes and dents, but I'm sure it can be fixed."

"But the wheel is all bent up! I saw it when you stuck it by the bridge!" I blared in frustration.

"Everything can be fixed," my father responded reassuringly. "Tomorrow we'll take it to Benny Maxwell. If anyone can fix it, Benny can."

That night in my dream I saw a dark cloud settle over our community, and bicycles of all shapes and sizes fell from the sky and floated to the ground. As they landed, Norman Donelson and his brothers smashed the wheels with long sticks. Sparks flew from the wheels and shot into the sky like shooting stars. Father ran around in circles, shaking his fist at the boys. Uncle Robert drove up in his pickup, screeched to a halt, jumped out, grabbed Norman by the seat of his pants, flung him in the box, and drove off. All the time the brothers were chanting "kiss me ass ...

kiss me ass." I woke up in a cold sweat with the bedsheets tangled around my head.

I came downstairs to the kitchen and was surprised to see my father sitting at the table and not at work as usual. My breakfast was ready and warming on the back of the stove.

"Eat up your breakfast and we'll take your bicycle to Benny's Repair Shop," my father instructed.

Benny was a small, thin man with thick wire-rimmed glasses who talked and moved slowly. His shop was impeccable and smelled of fresh orange-scented hand cleaner. His tools were neatly hung on a pegboard above a workbench. Nuts and bolts were stored in glass bottles suspended by their covers fastened to the underside of a wooden shelf.

Benny wiped his hand on his overalls and extended it to my father. "What happened?" he asked, nodding at my bicycle.

"The boy had a bit of an accident," my father answered. "Do you think you can fix it for him, Benny?"

"It looks a bit severe, but I can sure try," he answered with a smile.

Benny turned the bicycle over on its handlebars and seat and began slowly turning the bent rim, tightening and slackening various spokes. I was absolutely enthralled with each delicate movement of his small hands. I was expecting the wheel to have been wedged into a vice and forcefully pounded into place.

"What's that tool called? How will doing that straighten my wheel? Don't you need to hammer it or twist it?"

"The tool is called a spoke key," Benny responded. "Sometimes, the best results are obtained in the gentlest of ways."

He explained his technique, allowing me to hold the wrench and turn it.

For what seemed like forever, Benny twisted, turned, and tinkered. Finally, he surrendered, carefully replaced the small spoke key to its appropriate space on the pegboard, and spoke to my father apologetically. "Sorry, George, 'tis twisted too bad. I can't do a thing with it. I'll need to order a new wheel."

It was a long time before I got to ride my bicycle, and I never again felt the same about it.

When I was 12 years old my nose was badly busted. It happened one day while playing hockey on the harbour ice. A two-day mild spurt with rain and calm winds, followed by a deep freeze, had turned the harbour into a pool of quicksilver. It was a perfect mid-winter present from Mother Nature, and all of the community's aspiring hockey players took full advantage and stickhandled late into the evening. On this particular evening, as the orange glow of the sun reflected off the shiny ice, I stood squarely between two large rock goalposts, dutifully keeping guard. Norman Donelson, whom I had not seen previously that day, sauntered onto the ice in a pair of logans that looked two sizes too big for him and demanded a stick from one of the younger boys. He joined in the game on the opposing team by running after the puck. Ordinarily, on rough saltwater ice, this was not a serious disadvantage but, with smooth and slippery ice as it now was, he was as awkward as a duck on dry land. His frustrations soon got the better of him and he cursed loudly, calling for someone to pass him the puck.

Before I knew it, my nemesis was standing in front of me, unopposed. My initial instinct was to exit my post, but I stood as frozen as the ice on which I was standing. I was without any protective goalie equipment, for two reasons. First, it was a luxury not affordable to us at the time. Second, it was not really needed because the boys my age could not shoot the puck hard enough to do serious damage. Norman Donelson, however, was older, bigger, and stronger. He cocked his head to the side, squinted one eye, and looked straight at me. He bent forward to gain leverage and fired. The puck hit me directly on the bridge of my nose, and I went down, hitting the ice like a sack of potatoes.

When I came to my senses, I was being dragged over the ice with blood spurting from both nostrils, soaking my homemade jersey and leaving a trail of red on the white surface.

"My God, what happened? Is his throat cut?" my mother asked in a panic, as I was led into my house by two boys still wearing skates.

"No, Ma'am. He got struck in the nose with the puck," answered one of them.

When I saw the doctor later in the evening, he was not gentle as he gripped and twisted my swollen nose. "I don't think it's broken. Keep an ice pack on it."

Several days later, my mother saw fit to question me about my mishap.

"Who shot the puck?" she asked.

"Norman Donelson."

"Did he try it?"

"I don't know." I was telling the truth. I would never know, but I would forever have suspicions.

It took several weeks for the facial swelling to pitch down and for the bruising around my eyes to disappear. Years later, it took minor surgery to remove scar tissue before I could properly breathe through my nostrils.

At age 16, I graduated high school, which at the time meant successfully completing Grade 11. To honour the members of the graduating class, a special ceremony was held in the school auditorium. Each graduate was permitted to invite two adult guardians to the formal dinner part of the evening and one guest/date to a dance that followed. I was giddy with excitement when Peggy Thompson, the prettiest girl in town—in my biased opinion—accepted my invitation.

It was the first time that such an event had been held in our school, and it drew much attention. The auditorium was draped in colourful crepe paper and hundreds of balloons were suspended from the ceiling. The male graduates sported three-piece suits; the girls, fancy floor-length gowns and elaborate hairdos.

Norman Donelson, who had dropped out of school in Grade 8, was ineligible to attend on his own. He had not received an invitation from any of the girls. Nevertheless, he, along with one of his brothers and a few hard-cases from up the shore, showed up when the dance started, and relentlessly attempted to crash the party. Our teacher-chaperones spent the entire evening standing guard at the door and were subjected to persistent verbal abuse from the lurking scoundrels.

After the dance ended at midnight, I was happily holding Peggy's hand, escorting her along the gravel pathway away from the school when I heard a rustling noise in the low alder bushes that lined the path. Suddenly, Norman jumped out in front of us with arms outstretched, blocking our way. His brother and two comrades surfaced behind him.

Peggy and I halted abruptly and looked at each other, unsure of what to do. The silence was deafening. Finally, Peggy broke the stillness. "Excuse us, please," she said in a polite but deliberate tone.

Norman mimicked her. "Excuse us please ... thank you very much please."

The smell of homebrew hung in the still spring air like sour fish in a schooner's hold. I surveyed my surroundings for an appropriate escape route but saw none, other than doing an about-face and retreating. Had I not been with Peggy I would have done so, but my male ego surfaced and I jerked on Peggy's hand in an attempt to sidestep Norman's hulking form. As I did, he stuck out his foot and tripped me, pushing me from behind as I stumbled. I released Peggy's hand so that I wouldn't pull her down with me. When I hit the ground, I heard the knees of my dress pants tear, and I felt small stones bite into my palms. I looked up: Norman stood over me with both fists cocked.

"Come on, let's fight," he growled.

"That's it, Norm, give it to him good. Knock the shit out of him!" shouted his freckle-faced brother.

A wave of nausea swept over me, and an uncontrollable trembling sensation ran into my extremities. I knew I was no match for Norman and that standing up to face him meant taking a beating. Nevertheless, I looked at Peggy and slowly got to my feet to allow the inevitable. A greasy grin formed on Norman's lips, and he squinted at me the same way he had done when he fired the puck that had busted my nose. I clenched my fists, raised my arms in defence, and waited for the assault. But it did not happen. Peggy lunged at Norman with palms open and pushed him backward into a small group of students who had gathered.

"Go home, you asshole," she bellowed. "There'll be no fighting here this night."

Norman's jaw sagged like a youngster's soggy diaper, and his eyes popped open. He was stunned, but quickly recovered and sprang at his unsuspecting adversary, snarling like a surly dog. Peggy stiffened like one jolted with an electric shock and leaned her fragile body in the direction of her assailant, ready to defend. Norman halted. Not even Norman Donelson had the gall to attack a girl—especially in front of others.

"Shit on you!" he barked. "And piss on your puny boy-friend." Then he turned to his posse. "Come on, boys, let's go the fuck home."

Peggy affectionately turned to me, linked her arm with mine, and whispered in a voice as calm as the night, "Walk me home, please."

The light of a full moon bathed us as we walked quietly along the main road to Peggy's house and onto her front steps.

"Did you enjoy your night?" I asked shyly, looking down at my torn pants.

"Yes," she answered, leaning up and kissing me full on the lips. It was my first real kiss, and I felt a warm feeling surge through me and something melt inside. It would stay melted forever.

When I was 24, I made a career move that forever changed my life. Immediately upon completing high school, I had enrolled in a small-engine-repair course at the district vocation school in the city.

After my first visit to Benny's Repair Shop with my father when I was 10, I began stopping by Benny's place regularly. At first it was to check on the wheel of my bicycle, but, afterward, it was to watch Benny work. Benny always gave the impression that he enjoyed my company. No matter how busy he was he took the time to show me how things worked. In particular, he taught me about motors—how they worked and how to fix them. Before long, I was pulling apart and tinkering with anything that had moving parts. My vocational decision was not a difficult one.

My apprenticeship was served with a large well-known company in the city who hired me full-time after I completed my training. While my work was interesting and satisfying, my life consisted of a five-day workweek in the city and a four-hour commute around the bay on weekends to see Peggy, who had taken an office job at the local fish plant.

This routine continued for four wearisome years, until one day I received a telephone call from my father.

"Benny is retiring and selling his shop," he blurted out without salutation the instant I lifted the receiver.

The comment was not made in a manner to simply pass on information. His intention was in his intonation, and I immediately understood.

My heart jumped into my throat, and I paused to allow time for my brain to process the news.

Finally, I responded like a judge advising a jury in a murder trial. "Hang up. Call Benny right away. I may be interested. Tell him I'll discuss it with him on the weekend." And then, the call ended as abruptly as it started.

It was the longest week I had ever spent in the city. The thought of moving back home excited me; the idea of owning Benny's Repair Shop kept me awake.

"I knew you'd be interested, and that makes me very happy," Benny said when I visited him.

Benny's price was firm but fair. His only stipulation was that the name of the business was to be retained. To this I had no objection, and on the day of the summer solstice, I signed the final bank document that made me the proud owner of Benny's Repair Shop. My life instantly changed for the better. There were no more long commutes. I was living at home, eating my mother's home-cooked meals, and I was seeing Peggy every day. In the beginning, business was steady—nothing compared to what I had experienced in the city—but I was earning a modest living.

Then, one day, shortly after the first anniversary of my big purchase, a distinguished looking gentleman in a three-piece business suit entered the shop carrying a stylish leather briefcase.

"I'm looking for the owner," he declared.

"That would be me." I cleaned my greasy hands in a shop rag and initiated a handshake.

He received it like a long-lost friend and held it longer than necessary. Then he unclipped his briefcase and pulled out several photographs showing various shots of a small three-wheel machine.

"What do you think about this thing?"

"What is it? Looks like a motorcycle with two back wheels."

"It's an ATV—all-terrain vehicle—called a trike. Perfect for travelling over the bogs and barrens around here," he responded.

"Very interesting." I tried to conceal my skepticism.

"Would you be interested in stocking a couple? Test the market, so to speak. I think they'd sell well in this area once they catch on."

I was more of a mechanic and less of a businessman, so I hesitated. I needed time to deliberate, consult Peggy— and perhaps Benny—before making any major investment.

"Pure consignment," the charismatic salesman continued, sensing my apprehension. "You take no risk."

This, of course, put a different spin on things and made the decision an easier one.

"I'll try a couple—see what happens."

Shortly thereafter, two shiny red trikes were displayed on the lawn in front of my shop.

Instantly, they became the objects of cautious curiosity. Every man in the place walked around them numerous times, took turns sitting on each, and tested the springs by bouncing up and down.

Finally, just as I was considering returning the two anomalous ornaments to their rightful owner, Fred Macdonald came in with an envelope full of cash, purchased one of the machines, mounted it like Lone Ranger, and rode it home along the roadway.

Fred soon became the envy of the community when he demonstrated that his new trike was quite the workhorse and not merely a source of transportation. He designed a woods trailer, hooked it up to the three-wheeler, and pulled home the entire lot of firewood he had cut the previous winter. And he tied it to his 20-foot punt and effortlessly pulled it up on the community slipway.

The next week Matty Hunt, Fred's next-door neighbour, bought the second trike. Matty, who was just as ingenious as Fred, modified his old horse plow to fit the trike and tilled his entire potato garden as well as the gardens of all those living around him.

After that, the versatile little machines became as popular as indoor plumbing. They became essential to rural living, and everyone wanted one. I seized an opportunity and, with the help of my salesman friend, acquired a dealership franchise. Before long, every trike sold anywhere on our coastline had a Benny's Repair Shop sticker on it. Life was good.

As for Norman Donelson, he began making regular jaunts to Toronto around the same time I enrolled at the District Vocational School. He'd work a factory job long enough to qualify for Employment Insurance and then return home in an old souped-up automobile and proceed to terrorize the town by racing around, squealing tires, and blaring loud music. These escapades always ended the same way. Complaints flooded the local police station, and Norman would be arrested for anything from disturbing the peace to drunk driving. He'd make a brief court appearance, be given a hard talking to, and be released to disappear back to the mainland.

On one such home excursion, Norman was up to his old antics, racing around the town, burning rubber, and doing doughnuts, when he lost control of his late-model Chrysler Imperial, hit a utility pole, careened across the road, and crashed through the front wall of the post office. Unfortunately, Banfield Curtis, the night janitor, was inside scrubbing and waxing floors. Banfield was sent crashing through a panel of postal boxes, ending up with a concussion, two broken legs, and a ruptured spleen.

This time the judge had had enough of Norman's antics and slammed his gavel down hard, suspending

Norman's driver's licence and sentencing him to do time in Her Majesty's Penitentiary in the city.

The people were delighted that, finally, Norman had been held liable for his reckless actions. Their elation was short-lived, though, when Norman was released on parole before his victim was even discharged from the hospital. Jail time had done little to rehabilitate Norman, but it was not without consequence. He returned from prison with a jagged scar running from his left eyebrow to the corner of his mouth, and his left eye was glazed in a ghostly white film. This disfigurement only embellished Norman's devilish character and caused others to view him in the same dreadful way I always had. Rumours claimed that his glossy eye was actually artificial—that he had gotten into a fight with a fellow inmate and had been sliced with a homemade shank. Whatever the truth, Norman was deemed disabled and entitled to disability compensation. Consequently, he never again went away to work but stayed at home living on the public purse. He acquired a well-used trike from Johnny Thompson for three bottles of moonshine, fixed it up with parts from the scrapyard, and raced it around the roads at all hours of the day and night.

When I was 27 years old, I proposed to Peggy Thompson. She accepted, and we planned a late fall wedding. Peggy wanted the occasion to be special, with local flavour—especially for visitors from the mainland who were expected to attend. It was her intent to provide each guest with a decorative, souvenir bottle of homemade partridgeberry jam. It was my task to pick the many gallons of berries needed to facilitate her creative generosity.

Consequently, on one sunny Saturday afternoon in mid-September, I was on Backside Trail (the one that meanders along the rugged shoreline behind the community) picking the plump red berries that grew in abundance on the barrens near the cliffs.

I did not particularly enjoy berry picking, but on this day, I felt a serene peacefulness with my surroundings. The feel of the soft salt wind off the ocean, the smell of the tart berries, and the sound of them bouncing in my bucket planted me comfortably in Mother Nature's kitchen. All the time I visualized Peggy walking down the aisle of our little church with her wedding dress train swiping the floor.

As the afternoon grew late, the repetitive picking motion and the sound of the waves washing against the cliffs rendered me in a near hypnotic state.

I was startled out of my reverie by a loud racket that I instantly recognized as that of a poorly tuned ATV with a missing muffler. Norman Donelson's three-wheel rattletrap bounced over the barrens heading in my direction. A familiar fear quivered in my gut.

I noticed Peter Hutchings sitting on the seat behind Norman with a case of beer wedged between his legs. Peter, somewhat of a friend to Norman, was known as a bit of a drinker and a hard case, but, in my opinion, he was a harmless soul. In fact, his presence actually helped to ease some of my tension. It was obvious that the two were on a drinking excursion.

Norman set a course directly for me, and I was forced to step aside to allow the noisy vehicle to pass, while avoiding eye contact with either man. Nevertheless, in my peripheral vision, I noticed Peter giving a friendly gesture in salute as the ATV shot by me. Norman, on the other hand, focused straight ahead, making no attempt to avoid my heaping bucket of berries. The collision sent berries and bucket flying.

"Why did you do dat?" Peter shouted.

I could not make out Norman's response, but I clearly heard his infamous evil cackle explode above the sound of the noisy motor. The two shady characters continued on their way until they came to a small windswept thicket, where they parked the trike out of sight. Then, they cautiously climbed upon a jagged splinter of protruding rock, plunked the beer case between them and sat with feet dangling over the edge of the cliff. I watched as they drank one beer after another, ceremoniously smashing the empty bottles against the adjacent cliff wall.

The next morning, I pretended to be sleeping when my mother entered my bedroom and shook me. "Get up. There's something strange going on out along the shoreline! Your father has already gone to check it out."

I jumped from my bed and ran to the window. The road leading to Backside Trail was a beehive of activity. People were scurrying about and two police cars were parked at the end of the road with lights flashing—one perpendicular to the other, blocking the entrance to the trail.

"What is it? What do you think is going on?" my mother asked apprehensively.

"I don't know. Must be someone in trouble or hurt."

Soon, our telephone line heated up with call after call, relaying details of a terrible accident. Before long, and after making a few calls of her own, my inquisitive mother pieced together the details of the story.

Apparently, late the previous evening, Tommy Ivany had been hauling his herring net in the waters just off Backside Trail and had been steaming home close to the shore when he heard a loud roaring resonating from Bird Gulch. He manoeuvred his skiff through the narrow entrance of the gulch to investigate and saw an ATV bottom-up on the rocky shoreline, its motor racing. Unable to land at the bottom of the steep gulch, Tommy steamed home at full throttle and reported what he had discovered to the RCMP.

It was well after dark when the police arrived on the scene and after midnight before a rescue team with flashlights and ropes scaled down the face of the gulch. They found Norman Donelson's body on the sharp rocks some 50 feet from the ATV, his skull split open and his neck broken.

"How terrible," my mother proclaimed. "Poor Norman—what a dreadful ending."

I made no comment and mentioned nothing about what I had seen the previous day.

I quickly ate my breakfast and made my way to the site of the accident to see for myself what was happening. A crowd of onlookers—men, women, and children—were lined around the rim of Bird Gulch watching the recovery operations. I spotted my father and Benny standing on the far eastern side, from where they had a clear view into the gulch.

"What's happening?" I asked, sidling in between them.

"It's Norman Donelson. He ran his trike over the cliff and killed himself. Gideon White and some more of the fishermen from the east side are down there now trying to secure the body," Benny replied, shielding his eyes with his open palm to reduce the glare off the water.

I watched in awe as agile fishermen skilfully assembled a configuration of blocks and tackles from the top of the cliff to the toothed rocks at the water's edge. Then, smooth as a soaring raven, a black zipped-up body bag was hoisted up the rocky escarpment. A collective sigh went through the crowd when the rigid remains were retrieved and settled upon the mossy bank. Ironically, the bag was placed on a trike and escorted away by a police officer. A second officer shouted to the men below to also secure the trike, and the attachment cable was sent back down to them.

This was done, and a short time later a bulldozer was brought in from a nearby rock quarry, attached to the prepared apparatus, and Norman's mangled trike was salvaged.

The cause of the accident appeared obvious to most; nevertheless, Norman's body was sent off to the city for an autopsy and his ATV confiscated by the police for examination. Many residents came forward with information, reporting that Norman and Peter Hutchings had been drinking together on the day of the accident.

Several of them admitted to seeing the two buckos riding double, heading for Backside Trail. As a result, Peter became—as the police termed it—a person of interest, and an official investigation was launched. Peter was not arrested, but he was taken to the local police detachment and questioned at length. He admitted to having gone to Backside Trail with Norman to drink beer, but he claimed that the two had had an argument, and he had left Norman on the trail to walk home alone.

The inquiry went on for more than a week, and Peter was brought in several more times for questioning. Peter claimed that Garfield Eddy was working in his potato garden near Backside Trail that evening and had seen him walking the trail toward home. Garfield, however, had no recollection of having seen anyone.

"At least, I didn't take notice," Garfield declared.

The matter was now a criminal affair, and the entire community was buzzing with theories and allegations. Most felt that it did not look good for Peter.

However, the results of the autopsy and the ATV inspection led to Norman's death being documented as accidental—caused by the unsafe condition of the ATV and by the intoxicated state of the driver. Peter was officially cleared of any involvement in the death of Norman Donelson, but our small community was no different than most. Fingers continued to point in his direction and, from the shadows of dimly lit kitchens, accusations were whispered. Peter was, after all, an unsavoury character, and he did admit to having had an argument with Norman on that ill-fated day. Most believed that Peter knew more about the incident than he was letting on. Some even felt that he had gotten away with a serious crime.

I, on the other hand, did not share the community's sentiments. As far as I was concerned, it was not in Peter Hutchings's nature to deliberately cause harm to anyone, and I was certain that he did not have the mechanical aptitude to doctor an accelerator cable so that it would not release once depressed.

Sometimes, the best results are obtained in the gentlest of ways.

Boss Boyd

He was known as Boss Boyd. Half of the place loved him; the other half despised him. That didn't stop everyone from coming to his funeral. The little church was filled to capacity, and everyone sang their hearts out, while women dabbed at their eyes with tissues. I was there partly out of obligation. I had not been home in a long time, so I reasoned that a funeral was as good an excuse as any.

Opening my hymn book to "Abide with Me," I silently followed along with the words. The hypnotic drone of the choir and the off-key squawks of Evelyn Baker caused me to reflect about Boss Boyd, my hometown, and my boyhood.

When other helpers fail and comforts flee
Help of the helpless, O abide with me ...

Boyd had the good fortune to have been the son-in-law of Jacob Harrison, the local fish merchant and store owner. With nepotism alive and well, Boyd was the top boss in charge of operations on the wharf and in the fish plant. He decided whose fish was bought and when it could be shipped. He also determined who received the much sought-after jobs and who "got on," as everyone referred to the hiring practice.

Other than a few men who worked through the winter off-season doing mostly maintenance work, there were no permanent jobs at the plant. Instead, work was assigned daily, depending on the abundance of fish and the time of the year. Consequently, getting on was a ritual. Each morning men gathered at the entrance to the wharf and milled around until Boss Boyd emerged through the gateway in a chain-link gate. Then, in military fashion, the expectant workers formed a single-file line and waited for him to walk the length of the queue, abruptly pointing a forefinger at the men he wanted to perform particular tasks.

"Johnny, I want you to go splittin' ... Albert, salting ... Michael, in the dryer ... Sammy, out on the weigh scales ... Willy-James, you're stampin' boxes ..." and down the line he went until he had filled his roster. Each man knew the job to which he was assigned and immediately fell out of line and went straight to work, without further instruction. Those who were left behind gathered for a few minutes, made accusations of favouritism, gathered up their lunch boxes and other belongings, and sauntered home to return the next day, and the next, and the next.

In June and early July when trap fish were plentiful, and in late summer when the schooners returned from Labrador, extra men were often needed—sometimes more than were available. Thus, Boss Boyd was forced to hire schoolboys or to point a reluctant finger toward the likes of Heber Russell.

Heber was a short heavyset man who was unusually slow in the way he moved and spoke. This earned him the reputation of being lazy. Boss Boyd was desperate for workers when he pointed a finger to pick Heber. Mothers judged the abundance of work by Heber's routine. If they didn't see him returning to his little rundown house shortly after the 8 o'clock whistle started the workday, they assumed that he had been hired on, and rooted their teenage sons out of bed.

"Get up and get yourself down to the wharf. There's work to be had. There's no sign of Heber," they would say.

When Heber developed a neurological disorder in his early 40s and became confined to his bed for the rest of his days, the community attributed his laziness to sickness and accused Boss Boyd of being unfair to him.

Familiar, condescending, patient, free.
Come not to sojourn, but abide with me . . .

Heber wasn't the only person that Boss Boyd had been accused of treating unfairly. One time, there was a community uproar when he banned Millie Collins from the premises, threatening the Mounties on her if she returned. Millie, a single mother with a slew of youngsters, spent much of her time at the end of the splitting line, rummaging through the discarded cod's heads to collect tongues and jowls—delicacies she peddled door to door for much-needed cash.

Johnny Peddle, a bit of a prankster, was a constant source of torment to Millie, teasing her about having loose morals and making sexual innuendoes. One day he flicked a sound-bone and struck Millie between the legs. Millie considered this a vulgar assault and had had enough. She made for Johnny with her knife, threating to cut off his goddamn balls and would have done so had three workers nearby not wrestled her away.

Johnny was the best fish splitter in the community and claimed it was an unfortunate accident. Boyd sided with Johnny, claiming that Millie was a nuisance and a distraction to the workers and had no right to be on the premises in the first place. Most of the community sided with Millie, declaring that she was a poor hardworking mother, while Johnny Peddle was a braggart. I was much too young to have an opinion one way or the other.

Thou on my head in early youth didst smile,
And through rebellious and perverse meanwhile ...

Boss Boyd's house was located in a huge garden at the far end of town. We were his nearest neighbour. A long picket fence separated his property from ours—a whitewashed barrier that I had been told by my parents not to cross. And I did not.

As the hymn droned on, I saw myself as a young boy peering through the rough pickets at Boss Boyd's big lustrous white two-storey house, wondering what it would be like to live in a house like that. I recalled watching him drive his motor car—one of the few in the community—into his garden and park it neatly adjacent to his front bridge.

Vividly, I recollected the time he noticed me watching him and called out.

"What are you doing?" he asked with a smile.

"Nothing," I responded sheepishly.

"Do you like trout fishing, Billy?"

"Yes, sir," I answered.

"Would you like to go to Diamond's Long Pond with me tomorrow evening?"

"Yes, sir," I'd responded excitedly.

"Okay, you dig us some worms and be ready first thing after supper tomorrow. That's if it's all right with your mother."

The next morning, while the dew was still on the ground, I diligently dug in the potato garden in search of fat, juicy earthworms, placed them in a hole-riveted tobacco tin, and proudly handed them over the fence to Boss Boyd when he returned from work.

Diamond's Long Pond, the headwaters of a system of small rivers that emptied into the harbor, was about a 10-minute drive. I was more excited about the car ride than I was about the fishing and could barely contain myself as I carefully studied the way Boss Boyd gripped the steering wheel and pulled the gearstick.

It was the first of many fishing trips we took together.

I also remembered another time Boss Boyd called out to me. It was the last day of the summer recess and I was playing in my garden, my head filled with thoughts about returning to school.

"Billy, come here," he called.

I went to the fence.

"Are you excited about going back to school tomorrow?"

"I s'pose," I replied with as much enthusiasm as I could muster.

"Here you are, my son. A little something for you." He handed me a brown paper bag.

I was surprised, and unsure whether to open it immediately or to keep it for later.

"What is it?" I asked shyly.

"Well, take a look," Boss Boyd encouraged.

Inside the bag was a pale blue scribbler with a picture of the queen on the cover, a pencil case with three pencils, a pencil sharpener, an eraser, and a pack of Juicy Fruit chewing gum.

"Thank you very much," I said appreciatively.

"No chewing gum in school." He gave me a stern look.

"I won't," I responded.

"And Billy," he continued, "you make sure to keep up with your lessons and get all the book learnin' you can get."

I fear no foe, with Thee at hand to bless;
Ills have no weight, and tears no bitterness ...

Boss Boyd gave me my first job on the wharf when I was only 12. Fish were plentiful that summer, and every man who wanted work on the wharf got it—even Heber

Russell. Boss Boyd sent word to the school that there was work for the senior boys when they finished writing their public exams. Consequently, on the morning after my older brother finished writing his final exam, my mother rooted him out of bed at the break of dawn, packed a lunch box full of bologna sandwiches, filled a Thermos with weak tea, and pushed him out the door to join the hiring line. I shared a bed with my brother and was fully aware of the excitement. The thought of my brother joining the hiring line with the men on the wharf made me burn with envy. I decided to try my luck. Unbeknownst to anyone, I slipped out the back door and followed my sleepy-eyed sibling to the wharf and stood behind the watchman's shack, out of sight.

When Boss Boyd began moving along the line assigning various tasks, I quickly slipped to the end of the queue. Each person in the line was sent to work. My brother was assigned to the salt store to shovel salt from the bins. I was left standing alone, like a runt puppy abandoned by the rest of the litter. Boss Boyd smiled when he noticed me. Without speaking, he smiled and turned to walk away. Suddenly, though, he stopped and faced me. My heart fluttered in my chest.

"Does your mother know you're here?" he asked.

"Yes," I lied.

"Do you want to go water-nipper?" he asked.

"Yes, of course!" I answered, unable to conceal my excitement.

"Very good. Follow me and I'll get you the bucket."

The job of water-nipper was always given to a young boy. For a few cents an hour it was the water-nipper's job to collect drinking water from the government well and distribute it to the men at the various work sites.

"Hey, nipper ... over here!" they called, and the thirsty men filled the dipper that hung on the galvanized bucket and drank long and hard, smacking their lips when finished. I felt proud and important, and I made sure that the water was always cool and not one worker was in need of a refreshing drink. It was many years later when I realized that the purpose of a water-nipper was not to patronize the young boys, as I once believed, but to enhance productivity by keeping the men refreshed and on task.

Hold Thou Thy cross before my closing eyes;
Shine through the gloom and point me to the skies ...

I was 15 and writing public exams when Boss Boyd gave me my next job. I had sprung up like a bean sprout in a fertile pot and was just as skinny. Fish were again plentiful and Boss Boyd sent word to the school about an abundance of work. As she had done with my older brother, my mother encouraged me from my bed early in the morning, fed me a robust breakfast, filled a lunch box with sandwiches and fruitcake, and ushered me out the door to join the real world.

It was a calm, warm morning as I stepped into the roadway to make my way to the wharf. The putt-putt of boats returning from the fishing grounds echoed off the cliffs, and the smell of boiled bark filled the air. The line had already formed when I arrived. Several boys from my school were there, most standing next to their fathers. I stepped in next to Dave Bursey, a man whom I knew because he regularly came to our garden to draw drinking water from our well.

Boss Boyd moved down the line quickly. No one was turned away. When he approached me, he paused and looked directly at me. "Are you finished your exams?" he asked. Boss Boyd never hired a boy who was in any way jeopardizing his education.

"Yes, sir," I responded truthfully.

Looking past me he turned his attention to Dave. My heart sank.

"Dave, I want you loadin' the *Trader*—in the hold," he instructed. Then he nodded to me. "And take the lad here with you—show him the ropes."

My chest swelled and a smile formed on my face.

"Come on, my son, come with me," Dave encouraged, and I proudly followed a man three times my years and twice my weight to the wharf and aboard the *Coastal Trader*.

The *Coastal Trader* was a small schooner, owned by Jacob Harrison's firm, for the sole purpose of distributing supplies to the remote areas of the island and to the Labrador coast. The cargo on this trip was flour—100-pound sacks of white all-purpose flour—to be dispensed to the general stores along the coastline.

Dave and I joined a bunch of men on the deck of the *Trader* and waited for the 8 o'clock whistle to start the workday. The men, in overalls, knee-length rubber boots, and caps of various types, were laughing and carrying on. I noticed that most were smoking hand-rolled cigarettes. I was the only boy among them.

When the whistle sounded, the men scurried to form two lines—one in the hold of the schooner and one on its deck. Dave and I descended a homemade wooden ladder into the hold and joined a dozen or so other workers who had gone ahead of us.

A huge wooden chute was lowered into the hold and secured in place by a system of ropes—one pulling against the other to create tension. George Hunt, who appeared to be lead man in the hold, tested the chute by leaning all of his weight on it and bouncing up and down on it. "All good down here," he shouted up to the men on deck, his voice reverberating around the hollow chamber.

A man on deck shouted, "All hands ready."

Craning my neck, I looked skyward to see the schooner's boom swing into view with a pallet load of flour sacks dangling from it. The pallet was lowered to the deck next to the chute. Two men positioned themselves on either side of it. Together they grabbed a bulky sack and hoisted it upon the chute and gave it a little nudge. It came sliding down the steep incline, increasing in speed as it neared the end. George Hunt stepped to the end of the chute, caught the heavy bundle with a jolt, cradled it like a baby, and carried it to the far end of the hold and dropped it to the floor. Immediately, another sack was placed on the chute, and the line started to move. Each man in the hold stepped forward to receive a 100-pound sack and added it to the row that George had started. Within minutes of the operation starting, the air was full of powdery flour and the men looked like ghosts moving mysteriously around the dark belly of the schooner.

When my turn came, I marched forward with reluctance and looked up into a blue patch of sky at the far end of the chute. A shadow moved across the opening and promptly a giant sack filled the space. It was dropped and given a push to start it; gravity took over and it came sliding down. I planted my feet firmly and braced myself. The bulging bag hit me squarely in the torso, the air left my lungs with a gulp, my knees bent, my feet lifted, and I landed on the broad of my back with the huge sack on me. I tried to roll over but could not move. An eerie silence fell over the men. George and Dave ran to me and lifted off the suffocating sack.

"Hold the line!" George shouted up the chute.

"Hold the line," someone above echoed.

"Are you okay, my son?" Dave asked.

I stood up slowly, feeling my strength return but my embarrassment deepening. "I'm all right," I muttered.

"Why in the Jesus did Boss Boyd send a boy down here to muck sacks of flour almost as heavy as he is?" George complained.

"There's times I'm convinced that Boss Boyd don't have the sense of a louse," Dave added.

"Go up, my son, and ask to be put at something easier," George continued sympathetically.

"No, sir," I responded. "I wasn't ready. I can do it."

When my turn came again, I walked to the end of the chute with the determination of a bull mounting a cow. Dave Burry nudged up behind me and placed his hand on my shoulder. "We can take this one together," he said.

"Thank you, Dave, but I have to take it myself."

"There's nothing to be ashamed of, Billy—better and bigger men than you have had trouble handling a 100-pound sack of flour."

"I know, but I have to try." Then, with dreaded anticipation I inhaled and flexed my stomach muscles. I bent my knees to lower my centre of gravity and braced myself. The sack smacked me squarely in the chest, jolting me backward, but I hung on and did not fall. With a guttural grunt, I strained to straighten up and staggered to the pile. Lifting my torso in a way to give leverage, I heaved the lifeless sack atop of the others.

For the rest of the morning I took my turn, over and over, with each sack feeling heavier than the previous one. I counted the steps from the pile to the chute, and I silently sang country songs to distract my misery. By the time the whistle sounded to indicate lunch break, my stomach muscles burned and my legs and back felt an unbearable ache. It took all of my energy to climb the ladder out of the hold to join the men in the small lunchroom. Inside, the smell of tinned sardines and Vienna sausages nauseated me. I could not eat the lunch my mother had packed. Instead, I sat on a bundled tarpaulin, rested my back against the wall, and closed my eyes. The sound of words and laughter faded, and I drifted off to sleep. I was dreaming that I was writing a public exam and that nothing on the page was familiar when the whistle sounded, calling us back to work. George Hunt patted me on the back, sending a little explosion of white flour into the air. "Go home, my son, 'tis no need to torture yourself."

George's words swirled around in my head. I knew that no one would fault me if I did as he suggested. But I did not go home. I returned to the hold of the *Coastal Trader* and lugged one burdensome sack after the other until the 6 o'clock whistle sounded, ending the workday. I was numb with fatigue as I climbed the ladder out of the hold, and I stumbled when I stepped on the wharf.

I was walking along the road to home, laboriously placing one foot ahead of the other, when a car's horn startled me.

"Want a ride?" a voice called.

I turned to discover that it was Boss Boyd. I gestured to my flour-covered clothing. "I'm not fit."

"Don't worry about it ... 'tis only flour ... climb in."

I did not protest and settled in the front seat, the cushioned seats embracing my aching bones.

"How was your day?" he asked.

"Good," I answered, trying to sound energetic.

"So, you'll be back tomorrow?"

"Yes," I answered curtly, and the conversation ended.

I do not recall if I thanked him for the ride.

"You look like a sugar-coated candy," my mother said, chuckling aloud as I entered the house. "What were you working at?"

"Loading flour in the *Coastal Trader*," I answered.

"Sacks of flour?" she asked.

"Yes, 100-pound sacks."

"Alongside the men?"

"Yes."

"That was heavy work, wasn't it?"

"Naw. Not that bad."

"Well, I bet you've built an appetite. Go wash up. I got a nice pot of pea soup ready."

I was hungry and I devoured three heaping bowls of thick and delicious soup, with doughboys on the side. I wondered how much of the flour I had loaded that day would be made into doughboys. With my belly full, I laid back on the daybed in the heat of the woodstove and was soon fast asleep. Again, I dreamed. I was standing on a mountain of flour sacks; hundreds of men were marching around. They were pointing at me, laughing and chanting something in a language I did not understand. Mother woke me when it was time for bed, and I sank my body into the soft mattress and tucked the covers tightly over my head. I was relaxed, safe, and comfortable.

"I didn't expect to see you," Dave Burry said in the morning when I took my place in the hiring line next to him.

"Mother said Father was stubborn, and what is in the cat is in the kittens," I answered.

Boss Boyd came down the line in his usual manner. "Dave, back in the *Trader*. Billy, go to the head of the wharf to pick potatoes."

I was surprised and looked at Dave. He gave me a quick wink and a nudge with his elbow. I suspected that Dave, or George—maybe both—had had a word with Boss Boyd.

At the end of the wharf I was met by three boys from the north side whom I did not know well. Many burlap bags of potatoes were stacked under a tarpaulin-covered shelter. They were the leftover winter stock from Jacob Harrison's general store. We sauntered around, waiting for instructions. Before long Boss Boyd showed up and demonstrated how to cull potatoes, discarding the soft and rotten ones, while cleaning the solid ones and leaving them to be re-bagged later.

For five days I sat on an overturned bucket and picked spuds. When I got bored, I entertained myself by engaging in a smelly game of potato war with my new mates.

At the end of the five days all the potatoes had been picked over and work on the wharf ended. The summer fish glut was over and Heber Russell was returning home each morning with his lunch box tucked under his arm. I was never to work on the wharf again. The next summer was the year before I headed off to college; the fish saw fit to swim nowhere near our shores and there was little work for anyone.

Heaven's morning breaks, and earth's vain shadows flee;
In life, in death, O Lord, abide with me.

When I came out of church, I did not follow the funeral procession to the cemetery. Instead, I meandered down the lower road to the wharf. I stood under the *No Trespassing* sign and stared for a long time at the ruins of the old premises and continued to reminisce. I saw Boss Boyd strutting down the hiring line, pointing an authoritative finger. I heard thirsty men calling, "Hey, water-nipper, over here." I heard the whistle blow, and I heard the hustle and bustle of men running, carts rolling, and winches grinding. I saw men scurrying like ants, with arms full of dried cod and shovels full of coarse salt. I saw Heber Russell walking down the road looking weary and dejected. I smelled briny air and rotting potatoes. I thought about the men who were in the hold of the *Coastal Trader* with me that day so many years ago, most of them now real ghosts.

I wondered why the man who took me fishing to Diamond's Long Pond and gave me a new scribbler sent me to do such gruelling work. As I gazed on a rusty lock hanging on a dented chain-link gate, I understood why.

The Boxer

Alex Mason leisurely opened the double doors to his wooden shed and backed his black and white Chevrolet Belair into the sunshine. He had given it a thorough cleaning, inside and out, the day before. Now it was time for a good polishing. Stepping from the car, he reached in over the car's hood and made uniform circular wipes with a soft cloth, lifting the cloth at the precise moment required to avoid leaving even the tiniest streak. As he was buffing one of the chrome side mirrors, he caught a reflection of himself and leaned in to admire his unblemished complexion. He patted his cheeks softly, like a woman applying blush, and proudly flashed a fake smile, exposing a set of perfect teeth, one of which was capped with gold. *Not bad for a fellow from a place and time where teeth were scarce and skin was wrinkled with the sun and chapped with salt.*

The sound of tires on gravel and the sputter of a badly tuned motor caught his attention. He looked up to see a white pickup, with a homemade wooden box, speed around the corner and shoot past him. Brakes suddenly squealed and the vehicle skidded to a stop, fishtailing as it did. The driver revved the motor and rammed the transmission into reverse by popping the clutch. Gravel spit from its rear tires as the vehicle shot backward, like a giant squid sensing unsuspecting prey, and came to rest a few feet from Alex's prized Belair.

Charlie O'Brien, the driver, rolled down the window and leaned out. He flicked a cigarette butt that bounced off the hood of Alex's shiny car and rolled into the dry grass. Alex quickly stomped it out. The smell of beer and stale tobacco drifted from the truck.

"Whaddaya doin', Boxer, shinin' her up again? Why don't you get a diaper and put on her?"

Tommy Beckett, who was sitting in the passenger seat with a beer bottle wedged between his knees, leaned over and addressed Alex through the open driver-side window. "If you rubs Evelyn as much as you do that car, Boxer, she must be one happy woman."

Charlie laughed and tooted the horn, punctuating Tommy's remark.

Alex knew the two men in the pickup. They were among a group of local blokes who had been hassling him ever since he moved home. Charlie, especially, was bad news when he was drinking, and Alex felt uneasy anytime he was in his company.

"Why don't you fellows go on about your business," Alex said.

"I thought you'd jump aboard with us, Boxer, and we'll head to Sam's Place to pick up a case of beer," Charlie taunted.

"I don't like beer," Alex responded, directing his attention back to polishing his car.

"And I don't like you, Alex Mason!" Charlie snarled like a saucy dog being poked with a stick.

"So, the Boxer don't like beer. Well, pardon me," Tommy added.

"Naw, Tommy, the Boxer only drinks champagne, claims it don't make his piss smell," Charlie growled.

"Come on, Boxer, jump aboard with us, you don't have to drink any beer—just buy it. We'll drink your share. Spend some of that money you got tucked away," Tommy Beckett continued.

"Don't waste your breath, Tommy, the Boxer is too good to drink with the likes of us fellars."

"That's what he might think, but I'm willing to bet

that he wipes his ass the same way as you and me, Charl," Tommy retorted, snickering.

Alex dropped his cleaning cloth and, to avoid further confrontation, walked into his shed and out of sight.

"Ah, go fuck yourself, you snob. See ya at the time tonight," Charlie bellowed after him. He sped away, driving dust and loose gravel into the air. Alex waited until the pickup crossed the Bar Bridge and disappeared out of sight before re-emerging. "Bastards!" he said, as he carefully examined his car.

Alex Mason was only in his 40s when he returned from New York (which he incessantly pronounced "New Yark") with enough money to retire to an outport gentleman's life.

Alex was the youngest of nine children born into a fishing family that managed to keep food on the table but little else. Like his brothers before him, as soon as he was old and big enough to sport a set of oilskins, he joined his father in the fishing boat. Schooling was reserved for girls and a few boys lucky enough to have been born to elite families—and elite families were rare.

Alex, though, was not cut out to be a fisherman. Born three months premature, he was slight in stature and sickly, an observation not lost on a small community. The life of a fisherman was hard for the most able of men, but for Alex it was gruelling and unbearable work, and he was forever seasick.

Alex's father, Gus Mason, feared for his young son's welfare. "I don't know about Alex, he's just different … 'tis a sin to put him through it," he declared to his wife, Margaret.

"Alex is Alex," Margaret countered. "There's nothing we can do only be patient with him."

Nevertheless, when Margaret's oldest brother, Martin, came home to visit from the United States, where he had gone many years earlier to chase his dreams, Gus called him aside and had a word with him.

"Martin, I'm worried about Alex. He's not meant to be on the water and there's nothing else for him to do around here. How do you think he'd do in the States? Do you think he'd find work?"

"It's the Roaring Twenties, Gussy, and New York is booming. They're crying out for workers. People are flocking in from all around the world. He's a smart boy. He'll do just fine."

"Will you have a word with him, Martin?"

"I most certainly will, but what about Margaret? What will she think about me encouraging her boy to move away?"

"I suspect she'll be a little harder to convince." Gus chuckled. "But I'll deal with Margaret when the time comes."

Alex was sitting on the head of the wharf watching the sun settle into a still sea when Martin approached him. His uncle was a stranger to him; his fine clothes and proper accent made Alex feel inferior. All he knew about Martin was that he lived in a big city and was well off, and that each year, just before Christmas, a huge cardboard barrel filled with used clothes and other hand-me-downs arrived from him, by way of coastal steamer. Alex remembered the time he found a pair yellow dress pants in the barrel that fit him to perfection. In spite of smelling of mothballs, and thinking them to be stylish and up-to-date, he wore them around the harbour one night.

"Alex is wearing his mother's slacks," one of the girls commented, causing the other girls to laugh.

Humiliated, Alex hurried home, removed the pants and stuffed them between the floorboards of the fish store. He had learned that being different in a small community draws attention.

"Spending a little time alone?" Uncle Martin asked.

"I enjoy watching the sea at this time of the day, when it is calm," Alex replied.

"But not so much when it is rough and you're on it. Am I right?" Martin probed.

"Yes, sir." Alex feared that his uncle had been told

about his persistent seasickness and felt a twinge of embarrassment about it.

"I didn't like it much either when I was your age," Martin said. "In fact, I hated each time I pulled on a pair of oilskins. That's why I moved to the States—to get away from it. And, do you know what, Alex? I have not regretted it for one moment in all those years I've lived away. Someday, I will come back here to live, but there are times in this life that you need to broaden your horizons." Then, Martin proceeded to fill his young nephew's head with stories about an exciting life in the big city and about opportunities for fame and fortune.

Alex listened to the stories like he had when he was a little boy and had been told about little fairies that lived on big bogs and lured people from their homes on foggy nights. He absorbed it all with the same fascination. Before the conversation ended, his mind was made up. He would follow his uncle. He was not meant to be a fisherman. He had always known it, but now, for the first time in his life, he realized that there were other possibilities. He was going to show everyone in this town that he had some gumption. He was going to move away and make something of himself.

Alex kept his decision to himself until long after his uncle had gone. Then, one day at supper he shocked everyone. "I'm moving to the States," he announced with the conviction of a magistrate proclaiming a stiff sentence.

Margaret almost choked on her food, but she remained silent until she and her husband were in the privacy of their bedroom.

"That's Martin filling the poor boy's head full of idle bunkum," she proclaimed.

"Now, Margaret, don't be too hard on Martin. He only wants the best for Alex—as we all do," Gus responded.

"But Alex is too timid to be movin' away to be on his own. He knows nothing about how to get by in a big city. He can't even make a cup of tea for himself!"

"It's time to cut the apron strings, Margaret. Alex is old enough to know what he wants. There's nothing for him in this godforsaken place, only a life on the water, workin' like a dog—for what? Pittance. You know as well as I do, the boy is not cut out for that."

"Maybe not, but I can't see him movin' to a big city in a foreign country where things are altogether different than they are here. It was all right for Martin; he was bullish enough to bluff his way through and was lucky enough to have gotten a good job straightaway. For every one like Martin, there's dozens who fall through the cracks and end up coming home with their tail tucked between their legs. The boy has no education, and immigration requires that you be able to read and write to enter the United States. And, besides, where would he get the money for his passage? To pay the head tax? And to hold him over until he finds work?"

But Alex had made his decision. He was moving to the States and no amount of persuasion could change his mind.

What Alex lacked in physical stamina, he made up for in dogged determination. To get the money needed, he took to the water and heaved until there was nothing left to come up but green bile. He tried to teach himself how to read and write but, when the time came to depart, he had managed only to write his own name and to recognize a few basic words.

On April 2, 1925, Alex hugged his weeping mother, shook hands with his father and brothers, and said goodbye to the little town that had been his safe haven for his entire life. With emotions running the full gamut, a young and naive Alex boarded the steamer *Silvia* en route to New York City in the great United States of America. He was happy to be going but sad to be leaving; excited for the adventure but nervous of the unknown. His feelings, though, were soon swamped with seasickness as the

Silvia rolled in the big waves. By the time the big vessel docked, Alex was happy enough to stand on solid ground, regardless of what country it was in.

Alex quickly realized that he was alone in a strange world and needed to rely on his ingenuity to get by. Before official entry into the country was granted, all passengers were required to line up in single file. Immigration papers were authorized and stamped, bank statements checked, and a short passage was presented to be read. Alex was terrified. His immigration documents were in order, his head tax was paid, and his financial obligations were met. He never imagined that authorities would actually check his reading ability—the literacy requirement would be his downfall. He was mortified at the thought of being disallowed entry and forced to return home to the sneers of those who felt his move was foolhardy in the first place.

Reluctantly, he took his place in the queue and slowly moved forward. While others were engaged in boisterous dialogue, Alex remained silent and intensely focused, praying for a miracle. He reasoned that he would fake sickness, leave the line-up, and save himself the embarrassment. But, above the chatter of the anxious and excited passengers, he heard those ahead of him reading the words on the page that had been presented to them. As he was about to execute his escape plan, he realized that the same passage was being repeated over and over. He slipped to the end of the queue and worked his way forward until he was again within earshot of the passage being read. He strained to hear the words and to memorize them. This he did several times until he had committed to memory the entire composition. When his turn came, he presented his documents, held the paper tightly in both hands, and recited the piece of writing almost flawlessly, his eyes following meaningless words on the page.

Then and there, Alex Mason learned that no obstacle was too big to overcome—a premise that he used to his full advantage for his entire time in America. Within his first week in the foreign land, he secured a job at The Procter and Gamble Manufacturing Company as a silicator in the packing department. All he had to do was add sodium silicate to steel drums for shipping.

He found himself affordable living accommodations in a one-room apartment above a gymnasium and learned to use the public transit. Quickly, he learned the ways of the big city and settled into a life that was glamorous by comparison to the one he had known. He enrolled in night classes. Within the first year, he learned to read and write, not enough to be considered scholarly but enough to get by—and enough to advance him to a supervisory job, responsible for 65 men. He worked long hours and learned the value of money. When not working, he spent much of his time in the gym under his apartment, working out and learning the art of boxing. After years of this routine, Alex built up stamina and strength. He was known to have bragged that he had won long road races and had sparred with some of the biggest boxing names of the time.

After 25 years of hard work, Alex had saved enough money to officially retire to the land he missed. He came home to his family and a place that had changed little in the time he had been gone—a community that held no concept of retirement, that thought it silly for a grown man to jog through town in a pair of short pants. He also returned to rumours that he had made a fortune by purchasing shares in the company in which he had worked and that he ate in fine restaurants, dated high-class women, and had learned how to box. The latter had earned him the nickname Boxer and drew snickers from most of the town. Alex did nothing to dispel the rumours and embraced the image by driving his shiny car around the community on sunny days while sporting a tailor-made suit and patent leather shoes.

When he married Evelyn, the only daughter of a wealthy merchant from the capital city, the rumours festered into intense jealousy—especially from the likes of Charlie O'Brien and Tommy Beckett.

Alex gave the Belair a final buff, drove it back into the shed, and bolted the shed doors. Walking in the house, he found Evelyn preparing for the St. Patrick's Day celebrations—the one day of the year when the whole community came out for a soup supper and a dance that went into the wee hours of the morning.

"I'm not sure about going to the time tonight," Alex commented.

"And why not?" Evelyn asked.

"Well, Charlie O'Brien and Tommy Beckett have already started boozin'. They'll be looking for trouble."

"Tommy Beckett and Charlie O'Brien have been looking for trouble ever since they were old enough to hold a beer bottle, Alex, so I don't see why avoiding the party will change anything."

"I'll only provoke them if I show up there."

"But I've been looking forward to this for weeks."

"And I have too, but it's not worth it."

"Alex, come to your senses! You can't let the narrow-mindedness of this place govern your life!"

Evelyn was right and Alex knew it.

The smell of soup filled the air when Evelyn and Alex walked into the Parish Hall. The first sitting had already been seated, and the sound of slurping soup and clicking spoons created a lively and warm atmosphere. Alex scanned the crowd. There was no sign of Charlie or Tommy or any of his clique.

As soon as the second table was prepared, Stella Murphy came out of the kitchen and fussed over Evelyn and Alex as if they were special guests, escorting them to a spot near the head table, where the best desserts were arranged. Alex relaxed and ate heartily, instructing Frank Hiscock, who was seated next to him, that it was proper table etiquette to tip one's soup bowl forward and to scoop outward when drinking soup.

After supper was finished and the dishes cleared and washed, the tables were pushed back and the hall was prepared for the dance. The band, made up of local fellows who'd get together every year for the same event, got started with a traditional jig. Their next number was a two-step waltz, and Alex and Evelyn were first on the floor. Alex had learned some fancy dance steps while living in the States and was not bashful to show them off. He dipped and twirled Evelyn without missing a beat. Some applauded when the dance ended, others snickered and whispered in the low light of the room.

A slow country waltz enticed others, and the dance floor became crowded with couples gliding around the room, bumping into one another. As the evening wore on, paper bags full of home-brewed beverages appeared, and the place livened up. Those who didn't like to dance, did. Those who couldn't sing, sang along with the band. The hall was full of chatter, laughter, and music. Everyone was having a good time.

Just before midnight the outside door swung open, letting a rush of cool air into the room and the racket of the merrymaking out into the night. Charlie, Tommy, and a few other local cronies made a grand entrance. Charlie led the charge with his chest stuck out like a drumming grouse soliciting a mate. Alex was gliding Stella Murphy around the dance floor and did not notice them. Evelyn was sitting at the table by herself. Charlie spotted her and bolted for her with one arm outstretched and forefinger pointing. He did not ask; he simply grabbed her by the arm and yanked her onto the dance floor.

"Come on, let's have a scuff," he grunted.

Evelyn, taken by surprise, was unable to protest.

Charlie wrapped his big arms around the small-framed woman and pulled her tightly to him. The sour smell of alcohol and tobacco on his breath caused her to scowl and turn her head away. He led his reluctant partner around the dance floor until he spotted Alex. Then, the tormentor grinned tauntingly, firmed his grip on Evelyn, and dropped his left hand on her buttock.

Alex did not wait for the song to end, nor did he escort Stella back to her seat. He left her standing on the dance floor and walked directly to Evelyn and Charlie. The bait had been dangled, and Alex had bitten.

He took Evelyn's arm and attempted to pull her away from the big man's grip. "Come back to the table with me, Evelyn," he requested like one asking for a second plate of dinner.

"Hang on now, Boxer, the song is not over," Charlie voiced loudly, refusing to release his hold on Evelyn.

"Let me go, Charlie O'Brien," Evelyn requested, trying to work herself free.

"I said to let her go, Charlie, and I mean it."

Charlie hollered above the music, summoning an audience. "Look at this everyone: the Boxer is jealous."

Alex tried to wedge himself between the two, but Charlie locked his arms around his struggling prey and held on. "I'll not tell you again, Charlie ... let her go!" Alex's voice was stern, and his facial expression became as cold as a weather-beaten tombstone.

"And whadda you gonna do about it if I don't—you puny, rich big shot?"

"Big shit more like it," Tommy jeered from a group who had gathered around.

Alex did not speak, nor did he move. He locked eyes with Charlie, and the two stared each other down for what seemed like an eternity.

"Racket!" someone shouted, and the music stopped and the lights in the hall were turned on.

Evelyn broke free, raced to her table, grabbed her purse, and returned to her husband. "Come on, Alex," she said, tugging on his coat sleeve, "we're going home."

Alex's stance melted. Slowly he turned away from his adversary, placed his arm around his wife's shoulder, and began to escort her toward the door.

"Coward," someone shouted, and a dull murmur went through the crowd.

Charlie, fuelled by the alcohol that burned in his gut and by the attention he had drawn from the crowd, was not satisfied to have merely intimidated Alex. He lunged at him and pushed him hard from behind, sending him sprawling, headfirst, among the tables. There was sudden commotion in the building as tables collapsed and glasses broke. Women screamed, and scrambled out of the way. Charlie's bunch cheered and shouted encouragement. They wanted a fight.

"Go on, Charlie, give him a good shit knockin'!"

"That's it, Charlie, teach the little snob a lesson!"

Everyone else formed around the perimeter of the room, pushing to get a good view.

Sam Mackey, the chairman of the St. Patrick's Day Celebrations Committee yelled. "Leave him alone, Charlie. You're twice the size he is!"

His comment was lost in the uproar.

Evelyn ran to her husband's side and helped him to his feet, fussing over him and arranging his clothing. Alex looked dazed. A trickle of blood ran down his forehead and along his left cheek. Evelyn wiped it away with the back of her hand. Alex shook his head and shrugged his shoulders like a man struck with a chill. He inhaled deeply, sucking air through his teeth. He mouthed something to his wife. Evelyn stepped back and gently nodded.

Charlie stood alone on the dance floor like a giant. His shoulders squared, his chest projected, and his fists cocked. "Come on, Alex Mason ... let me knock some of dat gold outta ya mouth!"

As casual as a man getting ready for bed, Alex removed his jacket and handed it to Evelyn. Then, he strolled slowly and purposefully to face his attacker.

"All right, Charlie, you got your way." Alex angled his body like a man walking into a strong wind. He raised his left shoulder above his chin and lifted his fists high in the air, his elbows directly in front of his face.

"Blessed Jesus, 'tis Jack Dempsey!" one of Charlie's champions called mockingly.

Several in the crowd laughed.

"Go on, Charlie, he's askin' for it. Knock his goddamn block off!" Tommy shouted.

That was enough encouragement for Charlie. He pulled back his right arm taking leverage from his shoulder and threw a powerful smack at Alex's face. His knuckles smashed into Alex's guarding elbows, sending a piercing pain up his arm.

"You son of a bitch!" Charlie shouted, and he fired another punch with his other hand. Alex pulled slightly to the side and countered with a quick jab that caught Charlie on the tip of the nose. Water welled in the big man's eyes and blood ran from his nostrils. Charlie now boiled with rage, his temper out of control, and he launched a barrage of wild, uncalculated swings. Alex dipped and swayed like a buoy on a choppy sea, and the exasperated attacker missed his mark each time. Finally, in total frustration, Charlie threw himself at Alex in an attempt to tackle him, to use his weight to bring down the smaller man. Alex faked a step to the left, bounced back to the right, and came up underneath Charlie's arm, raking his knuckles down his rib cage and into the diaphragm.

The air left Charlie's lungs, and he gasped for breath. Alex had wounded his prey and he knew it, and he did what he had been trained to do. He struck again, quickly and repeatedly, his fists like the keys of a typewriter hitting paper. A gash opened above Charlie's right eye, and his face puffed up like a pudding bag dropped in hot steam. The big man was now dazed and defenceless. Alex held back and calculated his final blow. He caught Charlie on the bridge of the nose, sending a splatter of blood into the air. Charlie's knees buckled, and he went down with a thud. A collective silence fell over the hall.

Alex kept his pose, surveying the crowd in anticipation of other attackers. Tommy Beckett slunk to the back of the room. Everyone else froze. Carefully, Alex nudged Charlie's limp form with his foot. His eyelids fluttered, but he did not move.

The Boxer relaxed, dropped his arms, fell to his knees, and slipped his arm underneath Charlie's neck. He lifted the unconscious man's head into his lap and cradled it. He reached into his back pocket, removed a neatly folded silk handkerchief, and proceeded to gently wipe blood from the face of the man who did not like him.

The Christmas Visitor

Freezing rain had been decorating Roaring Cove since 2 p.m. Christmas Eve. Coloured Christmas lights crystallized into ice diamonds and winked flirtatiously at each other from bare deciduous trees and frosted upstairs windows. It was pretty, but it was snow that everyone wanted—especially the children—to stir that special Christmas spirit.

"It'll be slippery for the crowd making their Christmas rounds tonight, Uncle Mark," I commented, lifting the damper off his homemade steel-drum stove and throwing in a few shavings.

"Proper t'ing," retorted Uncle Mark. "'Tis time to give up gallivanting from house to house on Christmas Eve. Christmas Eve is time for family."

I knew that Uncle Mark's comment was uttered

impulsively and that he was actually thrilled with the thought of receiving his traditional Christmas Eve visit from the men of his community. Signs of senility had been evident in Uncle Mark for some time, and cynicism was an obvious one.

At 86 Uncle Mark was the oldest resident of Roaring Cove. A veteran of the Great War to End All Wars, he had been wounded in the Battle of the Dardanelles and left among the dead. He thrust nearly everyone's hands underneath his shirt to feel shrapnel embedded in his lower back—proof of his active war duty.

"War is a terrible t'ing," he would say. But in the next breath he'd add, "Some sport, though—knockin' dem Turks outta the cliffs. And the foolish buggers wore big red caps. Couldn't help but see 'em."

Aunt Mae regularly excused her husband's behaviour. "Poor Mark hasn't been the same since he came back from that big row overseas," she would proclaim.

Aunt Mae and Uncle Mark were the first people I met when I moved to Roaring Cove. One evening, shortly after supper, I heard a quiet rap on my front door. Through my kitchen window, I saw a small, elderly man with hunched shoulders standing on my front steps.

"You the new schoolmaster?" he asked, when I answered the door. "I'm Mark White—Uncle Mark to everyone around here. The missus asked me to come by and invite 'e down fer supper tomorrow evening. We got a fresh salmon, and we'd think it grand if you and your missus help us to eat it—'tis too big fer the two of us. I was in the Battle of the Dardanelles, you know. Wounded I was ... laid out with the dead. Got hit in the back. Here, feel."

I accepted the supper invitation and many more in the years following. And I spent countless hours in this old man's shed, watching his aged and crippled hands meticulously create model fishing dories, punts, and schooners. All of which he proudly gave away. For the past few weeks, I had been following his creation of a model church and, for the past hour, I had been watching him get more and more frustrated as he unsuccessfully toiled to fit the church with a tiny cross.

The church in Roaring Cove was 150 years old and badly in need of repairs. The maintenance committee had decided that a new church was needed, but Uncle Mark saw things differently. "A church is sacred," he said. "You don't tear it down as if 'twas an old fish store or something. I've seen my grandparents, my mother and father, and all of Roaring Cove that's gone before me, waked in that church. I was christened in it and so were my youngsters. 'Tis not right to tear down something that means so much."

Uncle Mark had shouted his concerns loudly, but they fell on deaf ears. Most of Roaring Cove thought a new church was a good idea.

One day he announced to me, "The old church. I can't let her go. I'm gonna build her again." As the tears welled up in his eyes, he explained his plan to build a model of the church.

And build it he did, a perfect replica, inside and out. From the beginning, I watched as every detail was shaped by the hands of this creator—this artist.

Soft pine was sawed into miniature studs, joists, and clapboard, and the exterior was erected, one piece at a time, exactly as had been done 150 years ago. Popsicle sticks were skilfully cut and molded into pews, and precisely split and shaped into kneeling stools. Matchsticks were sacrificially decapitated, stained, and made into altar rails. An empty sewing cotton reel was notched and hollowed into a baptismal font. Coloured cellophane was cut, glued, and framed into a mosaic. The church was complete except for the tiny cross.

"If 'twas wood I'd be able to shape it, but metal is harder to work with," Uncle Mark complained.

The cross that was so difficult to replicate had been

salvaged from a Portuguese fishing schooner that had been wrecked at the same time the church was being constructed. Uncle Mark's grandfather had told him about how he and the other Roaring Cove men had helplessly watched the little schooner fall victim to the devious and infamous Branescess, a sunken shoal, that had claimed her and so many others like her. The unsuspecting little vessel was in unfamiliar waters and had sailed directly over the shoal when it broke, sucking away her buoyant support, causing her to crash down on the hidden weapon.

I have often sat on the shore observing the behaviour of the Branescess when it was swelling after a big blow. The sea remains calm except for a gentle rising and falling like a human torso inhaling and exhaling. For 12 times it draws inward, expanding its liquid diaphragm; for 12 times it exhales a white froth onto Roaring Cove Beach, causing the stones to roar out the familiar guttural sound from which our little town acquires its name. On number 13, the Branescess sucks inward and holds until an explosion of jagged, black rock breaks through the surface.

It was number 13 that claimed the Portuguese schooner, impaling her on the sharp splinter of granite that rises like a decayed tooth from the northern end of the shoal. The lighthouse keeper sounded the alarm, but there was nothing anyone could do, only look on helplessly from the shore. The sea washed over the grounded victim, its wooden hull broken up, and it slipped into the watery deep. Only the forward mast and rigging remained entangled in the rocks, a stark testament to the power of an angry sea. Atop the mast, a small gold cross flickered in the sun.

When the sea calmed two days later, the Roaring Cove men searched the surrounding waters and shoreline for bodies, but none were ever found. No one ever knew how many lives were claimed. Nathan White, Uncle Mark's grandfather, pried the small cross from the mast and took it to the local clergyman, suggesting that it be placed atop the church steeple as a memorial to the lost sailors. This was the cross that Uncle Mark was working so hard to reconstruct.

"Why bother with it at all?" I asked. "Half the people around here didn't even realize it was there."

"But I knew it was there," he retorted. "That cross was as much a part of the old church as the centre beam—I'll come up with something one of these days."

"Well," I said, checking the fire to make sure it was safe enough to leave, "all the Christmas lights are on. It's time to give it up for today."

The freezing drizzle had turned underfoot into a smooth sheet of glass, so I linked up to Uncle Mark and helped him climb the pathway to his house.

"Come in fer a Christmas toddy?"

"Maybe later," I replied. "I still have decorations to put up."

I had just finished placing the nativity scene under my Christmas tree when the telephone rang. It was Aunt Mae and she was frantic.

"Come down quick!" she ordered.

"Calm down, Aunt Mae," I encouraged. "What seems to be the matter?"

"Hold ya tongue, my son! A strange man showed up at the door. Come down off the highway, he did ... lookin' fer a bed fer the night. Mark put him out in the shed and barred him in."

I sensed the panic in Aunt Mae's voice, so I wasted no time getting to their house.

As I turned into the gate, I saw Uncle Mark slowly inching his way over the slippery pathway heading for his shed. He was sliding one foot ahead of the other and hunching into the wind to shelter his face from the freezing drizzle. I thought he looked unusually feeble.

"What are you doing?" I asked. "You're likely to fall and break something."

"I'm old, but I'm no invalid," the older man retorted.

"So, what's this about a strange man?" I asked.

"Come quick and tell me what 'e thinks," Uncle Mark requested, tugging me in the direction of the shed. "Hitchin' a ride up on the highway he was when the weather turned sour. Came knockin' on the porch door lookin' fer a place to bide the night."

"Aunt Mae tells me you barred him in the shed. Why in the world did you do that?"

"Indeed, I did. You should see 'en. He got a blessed great beard and hair down to his backside."

"Where was he headed?" I inquired.

"I don't know. He didn't say. But I got this, just in case he gets out," Uncle Mark proclaimed, pulling a breadknife from under his parka. "I'll run 'en through if I haves to."

"Put that away, Uncle Mark," I insisted. "The poor man is probably innocent enough."

"I'm not afraid of 'en, you know. I was in the Battle of the Dardanelles, where 100,000 men were killed."

"Yes, Uncle Mark, I know. But this isn't the Dardanelles. This is Roaring Cove. Let's have a chat with him to see what he's all about."

As I approached the shed door, I noticed that Uncle Mark had nailed a piece of board diagonally across it and had taken Aunt Mae's clothesline prop and wedged it between the door-latch and the corner of the fence.

Giving Uncle Mark a quizzical look, I called out to the

man inside. "Are you all right in there?"

The reply was faint and muffled. "Who are you? Why am I locked in?"

Trying not to upset Uncle Mark, I explained, as best I could, that he had come to the door of an elderly couple, who had simply overreacted.

"But I didn't intend to cause concern," the captive man replied. "I only wanted a warm place to sleep."

"You can sleep *there* tonight," Uncle Mark interjected. "Nobody is gonna hurt ya!"

"Are you cold?" I shouted through the door.

"I am not cold now, but I do feel uncomfortable being locked in," the stranger replied.

"Where's the hammer?" I asked, kicking the clothesline prop from the door.

Uncle Mark paused.

"Come on Uncle Mark, it's Christmas Eve."

Reluctantly, he reached underneath the step, pulled out a hammer, and handed it to me.

The stranger was getting out of his sleeping bag when I shone my flashlight into the dark shed. He was dressed in black long johns and heavy woollen stockings. His hair and beard were extremely long and disarrayed. Shavings from the shed floor clung to him.

Locating the light bulb hanging above the work

bench, Uncle Mark screwed it into its socket. As the light flooded the shed, the stranger focused on Uncle Mark apprehensively, and I could tell that he was leerier of Uncle Mark than the latter was of him. I offered the stranger my hand and introduced Uncle Mark and myself.

"I'm Boo," he said, accepting my hand.

I waited for an elaboration.

"Just Boo," he added. Then he turned to Uncle Mark. "I'm sorry to have upset you, sir."

Uncle Mark smiled, and I could see that he was beginning to soften. "Dat's all right, my son. Where were you heading anyway?"

"Nowhere in particular." Boo had a soft, warm voice.

We carried on a conversation for several minutes. In spite of our prying for information, Boo made no mention as to how he had gotten to Roaring Cove or where he had come from. He spoke without an accent and made no reference to any place being home. But, because of his comments about our cold climate and being unprepared to sleep outside, I guessed that he was from someplace warm.

I decided that Boo was a threat to no one. "Get dressed," I instructed. "I'll give you a bed for tonight."

As the visitor pulled clothing from his pack and began to dress, I understood why Uncle Mark had reacted the way he did. Boo's clothes were eccentric and well worn, with a military flair. A faded, khaki overcoat extended to his knees and was tightened at the waist by a narrow belt. His pants were loose, with large protruding pockets. These he wore tucked inside a pair of high, leather logans, similar to those worn by local fishermen.

His tanned face was mostly hidden by long dark hair that fell loosely over his forehead and by an untrimmed moustache. His face was not without character. His cheeks were hollow, accentuating his cheekbones, and his eyes the colour of the Newfoundland sea—azure with a tint of green. He wore a silver chain with a large peace-sign pendant around his neck. When he brushed the hair away from his face and tucked it behind his ear, I noticed that three gold studs pierced his left ear lobe. From the bottom stud hung a tiny gold cross, attached by a fine gold chain.

As we were about to exit the shed, Boo noticed the model church resting on an overturned barrel in the corner. He walked toward it, studying the structure intently. After a silence, he turned to Uncle Mark. "You made this?"

Uncle Mark nodded.

"Tell me about it."

Uncle Mark lit up like the Christmas lights that were glowing outside and told Boo the history of the little church, from the time it was built to the decision to replace it. He explained about his campaign to save it and why he was building a replica. He went into specific details about the time he spent carving, cutting, and shaping, and he told about the cross that was needed for the steeple and the trouble it was causing him. Boo absorbed every word.

I interrupted when Uncle Mark abruptly changed the topic to the Battle of the Dardanelles and opened his parka and pulled up his sweater for Boo to feel his wounds.

"Come on, it's time to go," I said.

By the time we reached the end of the path, Uncle Mark had invited Boo to sleep at his house; he insisted that I come in for the toddy I had refused earlier.

A Christmas toddy at Uncle Mark's house traditionally consisted of a glass of sherry and a piece of Aunt Mae's special Christmas bread—a recipe she refused to share with anyone. In anticipation, Aunt Mae had three wine glasses laid out on the kitchen table and the bread neatly arranged on her silver Christmas platter. Uncle Mark spent his usual five minutes fumbling around upstairs before emerging with the wine bottle.

In the meantime, Aunt Mae fussed over Boo like she did all guests at her house. "Are you hungry, my son? Would you like me to make you a little lunch?"

Boo politely refused, opting for the bread and wine

instead. As we ate and drank, Boo relaxed and engaged in easy conversation. He was interested in our land and questioned Uncle Mark and me about the ways and customs of our people. Uncle Mark was explaining resettlement when a sudden ruckus rocketed from the bridge—bawling, shouting, and stamping of feet. Before anyone could move, the door burst open and 10 slightly intoxicated men crowded into Aunt Mae's tiny kitchen. All eyes fell on Boo.

These were the men from Bakeapple Marsh Road— the Spurrells, Greens, Temples, and Sheppards. They were the ones who started the Christmas celebrations in Roaring Cove each Christmas Eve. It began with Peter Spurrell going to John Green's house for a Christmas drink. Peter and John then went to Luke Temple's, and it continued from there. They visited every house with a light on and picked up any man whose wife would allow him to accompany them. In the early Christmas morning hours, when they ended up in the lower end of Roaring Cove, there were 20 or so well-partied-out men.

They were not partied out yet, though, and they slapped their heavily rubbered feet on the canvas-covered floor to the sound of a lone harmonica. They hooted and hollered and sang at the top of their lungs. Before I knew it, I was pulled onto the floor. Uncle Mark and

Aunt Mae were already being swung from man to man. I looked toward Boo. He had retreated into the corner and Hayward Green and Luke Temple were reaching for him. He raised his arms in resistance, but each man grabbed an arm and hurled him onto the floor. His face showed shock and fear as he was swung in circles among the dancers.

Abruptly, the music stopped and there was a call for glasses as flasks of various kinds of liquor appeared from inside pockets. Boo retreated to his seat in the corner like a frightened puppy as the men filled their glasses. I inched my way over to him and explained that he was witnessing an old Christmas tradition and that there was nothing to fear.

"Give our visitor a glass, I pours him a drink!" Hayward Green shouted.

Hayward poured Boo a hefty grog.

"Merry Christmas to ya, my son," several of the men chorused.

Every man in turn toasted Boo, offering season's greetings and welcoming him to Roaring Cove. Before long, as a result of the hospitality or the effects of the alcohol, Boo was enjoying the festivity. He laughed louder than anyone when Jobie Rogers told the story about Jonas Pickett's trip to the lumber woods, and he applauded with enthusiasm when Ralph Sheppard performed a recitation.

For about an hour the music, stories, and recitations went on. Then it was time to move along to another house. I came up with a feeble excuse for not joining in the merriment and was teased about being henpecked. Boo was also invited to make the rounds and considered doing so.

"Should I go?" he asked me.

"Well, you have a warm bed for the night right here. If you go with this crowd, there's no telling where you'll end up," I answered.

"I think it wise for me to remain here," he concluded.

I agreed with his decision but made no further comment.

After the men left, and it was time for me to go home, Aunt Mae presented me with Christmas gifts—a pair of hand-knit trigger mitts for me and one of her special Christmas breads for my wife.

"When are you going to include the recipe with this bread?" I teased her.

"The Christmas before I die," she retorted with a chuckle as she disappeared into her knitting room off the kitchen.

She emerged with a small bundle wrapped in Christmas paper. "And this is for you, my son," she said offering Boo the package.

Boo accepted the gift with a smile. "God bless you," he stated.

Slowly, he unwrapped a knitted scarf and a matching stocking cap with a large fuzzy tassel.

"To keep you warm on your travels," Aunt Mae said.

Shortly after, I bid everyone goodnight and walked home, contemplating the events of the evening. The freezing rain had turned to snow. Large fluffy cotton balls were floating softly to the ground and settling into a white blanket of memories. It was the magical time of Christmas.

On Christmas morning the snow was still falling, and I awoke to the sound of the church bell ringing through the still air. We attended the service and returned home to open our gifts and make phone calls to family members. The aroma of turkey filled the house before I telephoned Aunt Mae and Uncle Mark to wish them a Merry Christmas and to check on Boo.

Aunt Mae answered the phone, as she always did.

"Merry Christmas to you, Aunt Mae ... and to Uncle Mark and Boo as well."

"Thank you, and to you and your wife also," she responded.

"So, will Boo be staying for Christmas dinner?"

There was a long pause before she spoke. "Hold ya tongue! I don't know what to make of it."

"What do you mean?"

"Well, we figured on him, at least, having Christmas dinner with us—perhaps even spend another night. We had such a lovely chat last night after you left. But, when we got up this morning, he was gone."

"Gone?" I sensed the bewilderment in her tone.

"Yes, he was gone. Vanished. Not a sign of him ever having been here."

No one in Roaring Cove ever saw or heard of Boo again.

A raging snowstorm had been blasting Roaring Cove since early morning on New Year's Eve. A strong northwesterly wind was causing the snow to twist and twirl in the air before settling in corrugated patterns. I had just returned from the woodhouse with a load of firewood when the telephone rang. It was Aunt Mae.

"Mark wants you to come down to the shed," she said, clearly excited. "He got something he wants to show ya."

I left my bundle of firewood on the wood-box and hurried through the snowdrifts to Uncle Mark's shed. As I entered his gate, I noticed smoke rising from the rusty funnel. It was being caught by the wind and drifting snow and was being baffled downward as if it were trying to make its way back to the place from whence it had come.

Uncle Mark was standing over the stove, stoking the fire.

"Not a very good night for the crowd at the New Year's parties," I commented, stomping the snow off my boots.

"Proper t'ing—time fer 'em to give up that trash of gallivanting around on New Year's Eve."

"What did you want me for?"

Uncle Mark hooked his bony fingers into my coat sleeve and led me to his workbench, where his model church was now lying.

"I came out here this morning, after breakfast—the first time since Christmas Eve. I noticed straightaway that my church was moved over here in the light of the window."

"Now look here," he said, twisting the church and pointing to the steeple.

A tiny gold cross had been mounted there. It was in the same proportion to Uncle Mark's model as the real cross had been to the old church. When I examined it more closely, I could see that it was a perfect replica of the original, except for a tiny hole at the top, where it had been attached to a tiny fine gold chain.

The Last Shot

Dan Mathew's luck had totally disappeared. It was evident when, for the second year in succession, he drew Taylor's Rock, the worst fishing berth on the coast. The Useless Rock, as it was referred to by local fishermen, was true to its reputation and had given Dan miserable catches again this summer. Each time he pulled his traps he caught barely enough fish to make a good meal, while the other fishermen were filling their boats to the gunwales. When catches did not improve by mid-July, Elmar Short, Dan's share-hand, did something considered reprehensible among fishermen—he left Dan to join a luckier boat from a neighbouring community.

"I don't want to leave you shorthanded, Dan, but I have six mouths to feed."

"Do what you have to, Elmar. I'd think less of you if

you didn't put your family first," was Dan's only comment.

If that wasn't bad enough, the next time Dan pulled his largest cod trap he discovered a hole the size of a dump truck ripped through the leader—he suspected a whale. With only himself to pull the gear ashore and do the mending, the summer trapping season was nearly over before he got the trap back in the water. A miserable failure—not nearly enough earned to put his credit back in good standing with A.C. Briffett, the local fish merchant.

A.C. Briffett and Sons, like all merchants, operated on a barter system, where fish was traded for food and supplies. Advances were granted one year for the next, leaving the fisherman more or less perpetually in debt. Years when the fish remained offshore, or if a particular fisherman had a poor season, the merchants opened their books, extending the credit. This was considered a generous and necessary gesture, but there were limits, and Dan had reached his the previous March. Dan and his then 11-year-old son, Freddie, met with Mr. Briffett and pleaded for an extension, but the meeting did not go well. Freddie witnessed the older man slam shut the ledger and sternly tell his father that he was cut off. Dan and Old Briffett stared at each other for what seemed like forever, and Freddie remembers noticing the muscles in his father's arms tightening and the sinew in his neck twitching. He will never forget the words his father muttered under his breath as he left. "Not in my lifetime will I ever ask that son of a bitch for anything." It was the first time Freddie had ever heard his father curse, or, for that matter, even have anything negative to say about another person.

What Dan Mathews lacked in luck, he made up for in enthusiasm and work ethic. He was determined to salvage the fishing season by working late into the fall, setting trawl lines and working hook-and-line. The fish were large in the fall so, with any luck at all, he figured he should be able to catch enough to get him through the winter.

But Mother Nature was in a cantankerous mood and blew one savage storm after another, causing the winds to rage and the seas to swell dangerously. Dan was forced to stay ashore.

Dan's wife, Mary, who was just a few weeks pregnant, held two-year-old William in her arms and, from her kitchen window, watched Dan's punt tear at its mooring like a tethered pony trying to break free. She cursed the elements—but did so silently, as not to upset the deities and bring even more bad luck.

Freddie sensed his father's anxiety and tried to help out. He worked alongside his father harvesting the vegetables, picking flour sacks full of partridgeberries, and cutting loads of firewood—all in preparation for a long, hard winter.

Christmas was a meagre time. No fresh coat of paint on the parlour walls to welcome a Christmas tree. No bottle of spirits from the city to record in the liquor book. No keg of homebrew beer tucked away behind the kitchen woodstove. No smell of spicy cakes permeating from the pantry. No toys from the mail-order catalogue for little William. No non-essential presents for 12-year-old Freddie. No pretty dress or shiny shoes for Mary.

At the stroke of midnight on New Year's Eve, Dan held his old breechloader snug to his shoulder and welcomed the new year by firing a shot into the night sky. It began an eruption of gunfire that split through the silence and reverberated off the cliffs, startling every dog in the place to burst into a symphony of barks and howls. "Things will be better in the new year," he announced to Mary, sniffing at the gunpowder in the frosty air.

Dan's optimism was short-lived. A mid-winter flu epidemic invaded the community like a pack of hungry huskies. Entire households were totally disabled. The very young and aged were especially vulnerable—four funerals in as many weeks. Dan's elderly mother had been one of them, and two-year-old William had been coughing and feverish for weeks. Mary, now heavy with child, was wearing herself down. "There's just not enough substance in fried dough and salt fish," she declared.

The winter dragged on like a Good Friday church service. Storm after storm blasted the coast as it had done in the autumn, shaking Dan's saltbox house on its rock foundation. Drafts crept through unputtied seams around the windows and doors, causing pretty frost patterns to form on the inside of bedroom windows. Even when the wind rested, the snow continued to fall. It choked off roads and pathways and piled high on rooftops and overturned punts. Getting about was arduous and dangerous, and routine winter activities were interrupted or completely abandoned. Next winter's firewood would have to be cut in the spring, or the following fall and burned green.

March was called the hungry month, for good reason. What little provisions there had been were already used up, and the weather continued to be unaccommodating. The days had lengthened, but wet snow laced with freezing drizzle stuck to everything like hot peas to a pudding bag. Dan ignored the dangers of the ice-encrusted snowbanks and the snow-covered crevices to search the rugged shoreline, hoping to shoot a saltwater bird or perhaps a seal—anything to put something fresh on the table.

When he found the gulches empty of game, or chock full of slob ice, he tucked himself away in a bird blind constructed of loose rocks and gravel, plastered together with wet snow. There, he patiently waited for hours, hoping for a target to fly or swim within range, but each day he returned home empty-handed.

When school recessed for the Easter holiday, the days had noticeably softened, so Dan allowed Freddie to accompany him on his hunting excursions. Freddie cherished this time spent with his father and learned about things that a 12-year-old growing up in a rural setting fancied. He absorbed every word when Dan told him stories about hunting adventures, about the times when tasty seabirds were plentiful, and when he killed six ducks with one shot. Sometimes, Dan allowed Freddie to carry the old breechloader and taught him how to shoot it: "Never point a gun at anything you don't want to kill," he began. "Hold her tight to your shoulder, else she'll knock you on your arse and leave your arm black and blue. Don't ever rest your cheek on the stock unless you want to lose an eye. When taking aim, line up the tip of the barrel with the hammer. If the bird is on the wing, make sure you aim ahead of it."

Freddie held his breath each time a diving pigeon or a flying merganser was spotted, and his heart pumped wildly watching his father pull back the hammer and pose himself in preparation for a shot. But his excitement was to no avail. The persistent wind kept the birds too far offshore and out of reach.

Sometimes, in desperation, Dan took a wild shot, hoping that a stray pellet would reach its target. Even a missed shot broke the monotony of the long, cold wait, and it caused Freddie to explode with excitement.

One day, Dan was spinning a yarn that had Freddie spellbound when two black ducks flew directly over the blind, taking both father and son by surprise. In a frenzy, Dan grabbed the resting gun, pulled back the hammer, took aim, and fired. The blast shook the makeshift walls of the shelter, and the two birds tumbled from the sky like a pair of old shoes dropped from a rooftop.

Freddie jumped to his feet yelling ecstatically, "You got them, Dad! Both with one shot!"

Dan grabbed the bird jigger, and the two hunters bolted from the shelter and scurried over the slippery rocks to the water's edge. But the curse of Macbeth seemed to have adhered itself to Dan. Both birds had fallen into the breaking surf and were being sucked out to sea by the retreating undertow. Dan vigorously tossed the buoyant bird jigger with its attached fish hooks, but each attempt fell short and neither bird could be retrieved.

Young Freddie watched in disbelief as a nutritious meal floated away to be devoured by scavenging seagulls. In spite of his attempts to restrain them, tears welled in his eyes and followed one another down his cheeks.

"That's all right, son. You'll never get them all. There will be more birds," Dan said, wrapping his arm around his son's shoulder, guiding him back to the blind.

Dan picked up his breechloader and reached into his ammunition bag to reload it. Much to his dismay, he discovered that only three cartridges remained. Dan tipped the bag bottom up and shook it vigorously.

"What's wrong?" Freddie asked.

"There's only three shells left," Dan answered, looking puzzled.

"What does that mean?"

"It means the end of the bird hunting for a while."

"But you can load more when you get home."

"Can't —I used up all of the caps and gunpowder when I loaded the last lot. There's nothing left only a handful of shot, and they're not much good on their own."

Freddie picked up the ammunition bag, pulled apart the drawstring and peeked inside like a trapper checking a baited trap. When he was satisfied that the bag was empty, he looked into his father's eyes. "We can get more caps and powder."

"Caps and gunpowder cost money, Freddie. And money is one thing we don't have."

"Well, we still have three shells left. We just have to be careful. Make sure each shot is a sure one," Freddie added.

"No, Freddie," Dan responded. "We have only three shells. They have to be saved in case of an emergency."

Again, Freddie felt his emotions swell. He swallowed a lump that had risen in his throat but said nothing. *In case of an emergency.* What did it mean? The distraught boy wondered, but he did not ask.

Silently, he watched his father pocket the three remaining shells, lash his gun and ammunition bag over his shoulder, and leave the blind. Like a loyal servant, he followed an elongated shadow over the ice-encrusted rocks and snowy paths to their house. All the while, seagulls, as hungry as he was, soared high above them, squawking incessantly.

When Dan entered his house, he did not put the gun behind the porch door as was the usual practice when he knew that he would be using it again in the near future. Instead, he wiped it dry with an oily rag and hung it on the wall above the kitchen stove. He removed the three cartridges from his coat pocket, wiped them with the same rag, and dropped them in a small porcelain dish on the mantle.

"Well, the hunters are home early. No luck again today?" Mary questioned rhetorically.

"We ran out of shells," Dan answered abruptly, pulling the steeping teapot from the stove and pouring himself a cup of steaming tea. Little William ran to him and climbed onto his lap. Dan poured tea from his cup into his saucer, picked up a loaf of homemade bread from the table, cut off a thick slice, soaked it in the tea, and fed it to his young son.

"Today, Dad knocked down two ducks with one shot, but they fell into the water and we couldn't get them," Freddie interjected dispassionately.

Mary furrowed her brow. "It would have been someone else's luck if they had fallen on land. What did we do to deserve such poor luck?"

"We did nothing, Mary. It's only a matter of time before things will change, you'll see."

"It's like Uncle Paddy Critch always says, 'When you think you're on the pig's back, you're really up his arse,'" Mary declared.

"We can't think that way, Mary. We have to say, when you think you're up the pig's arse, you're really on his back."

"Pig's back or arse, I'd welcome either on that table with a bit of gravy poured over it," Mary insisted.

Dan chuckled, not at the wit of her comment but to

ease the mounting tension and avoid another argument—an argument that he knew would create a smothering tension. Without further remark, Dan finished his tea in one long slurp, set little William on the floor, and went upstairs. After what seemed like a long time, he re-entered the kitchen dressed in his best clothes. It was obvious that he was going out.

"Where are you going?" Mary looked puzzled.

"Nowhere in particular," he mumbled mildly, fetching his fedora from a shelf above the coat rack.

Mary knew her husband well enough to know that, when he was vague like this, there was something on his mind that he did not want to discuss, so she did not probe.

"I suspect he's gone to see Mr. Briffett," she commented optimistically to Freddie when Dan had left the house.

"Mr. Briffett? Why would he do that?" Freddie asked.

"To request another advance, so we can put some solid food on the table."

Freddie did not argue with his mother, but in his heart, he knew that she was mistaken. He had been present the last time his father visited Mr. Briffett, and he clearly remembered the tension between the two men, and he recalled his father's parting comment. He knew that his father was a proud man who would not allow himself to beg—regardless of the situation.

It was almost dark before Dan returned home. The familiar smell of salt fish met him in the porch.

"What did he have to say?" Mary asked as soon as her husband came through the door.

"Who are you referring to, Mary?"

"Mr. Briffett. You went to see Mr. Briffett, didn't you?"

"No, Mary. I certainly did not go to see Mr. Briffett. Briffett made his position perfectly clear the last time I visited him. There was no point going again."

"Where were you, then?" she asked, looking perplexed.

Dan softened his composure to that of a schoolboy requesting a trip to the toilet. He reached out and held both of Mary's hands. "I went to see Captain Matt Sampson."

"Captain Matt—the sealing captain?" she repeated with a look of surprise. "What on earth for? Don't tell me you are going to the ice again."

"Yes, Mary. I've signed on with Captain Matt to go sealin'."

Mary dropped Dan's big hands as if they were hot plates taken from a heated oven. "Damn it, Dan! You promised me you'd never go sealing again."

"I know I did, Mary, and I understand how you feel. I'm not big on it either, but what else is there? The youngsters are starving. They look like thole-pins. We need something to tie us over until I can get back on the water—until my luck changes. What else was I to do?"

"You could have gone to see Mr. Briffett—anything other than that godforsaken sealing racket."

"I don't beg, Mary," Dan snapped. "Old Man Briffett turned me down flat. Don't you remember that?"

"But that was a year ago. Things are different now. Everyone has had their share of hardship with this bloody winter and that awful flu. You're not the only one looking for an advance. Mr. Briffett is not a mean man, Dan. He would understand if you explained our situation."

"I don't have much, Mary, but I still have two good hands and a strong back that can do a day's work, and, above anything else, I still have my pride." Dan tapped his index finger into his chest like a needle bobbing in a sewing machine. "I'd rather freeze to death on an ice floe than give Old Briffett or anyone else the satisfaction of seeing me beg for handouts."

Freddie sensed the rising tension and moved to the far end of the daybed, behind the kitchen stove.

"You call it pride, Dan Mathews, but I call it bloody stubbornness and nothing more. And freeze to death is exactly what might happen. You wouldn't be the first one, would you?"

"I don't like it, Mary. I told you that. But you can't

continue to live in the past. What happened six years ago is over with and done!"

"Time forms scabs, Dan, but it doesn't heal sores. I lost my father and brother at that goddamn sealing racket, and only by the grace of God I didn't lose you. And for what? To make someone else rich? I live with the loss every day of my life. How can you say that it's over and done with?"

"Sometimes we have to make sacrifices, Mary, and this is a sacrifice I have to make for my family."

Mary stiffened as she glared at her husband. "Then why not sacrifice your damn pride?"

"I don't want to fight about this, Mary."

"And, I don't want to lose my husband and be left to raise three children on my own." Mary burst into tears, turned, and fled up the stairs to her bedroom. Dan was left standing in the middle of the kitchen floor like a deserted warrior.

Young Freddie emerged from his place of refuge and came to Dan's side. He felt an urge to hug his father like he used to do when he was younger, but instead, he tugged on the sleeve of his jacket to catch his father's attention. "It will be all right, Dad, things will get better like you say they will," he declared in the most mature voice he could find.

Dan understood Mary's position and he empathized. He had first gone to the ice when he was a teenager and knew firsthand the consequences and the dangers of the hunt. Sealing meant weeks of torturous, dangerous, dirty work harvesting seals on floating ice floes that were continuously moving. If a sealer was lucky, he would come home with a few dollars and a dozen or so fresh seal flippers. If conditions were adverse, he'd come home empty-handed—or, perhaps, not come home at all. Each year dozens of men perished on the ice floes or were swallowed up by an unforgiving sea.

Six years earlier, Dan, along with Mary's father and oldest brother, had signed on the newest vessel in the fleet. With its powerful engine and steel structure, a bumper trip seemed promising. But, on a day in early April, an unexpected spring blizzard blew in with savage strength. Wet sloppy snow driven by gale-force winds reduced visibility to zero, and the majority of the crew became separated from the ship. Dan spent eight hours lost and freezing, but luckily, just as darkness was settling and hope running out, he heard the ship's whistle penetrating the blackness, summoning its crew. He followed the shrill sound through the blinding snow and boarded his ship, shivering like a pronged flatfish—as much from fear as from the numbing cold. Mary's father and brother were not so lucky. They, along with 10 other shipmates, were never seen again.

Every detail of that horrible event was still vivid in Dan's mind when he decided to break his promise to his wife and to himself to go sealing again. Consequently, his decision was made after anguished reflection. Nevertheless, each time he looked at little William's frail frame and Mary's skinny arms and protruding belly, he rationalized his choice.

On a warm spring day, Dan hugged little William tightly, firmly shook hands with Freddie, lovingly kissed Mary, threw his duffel bag on his back, and, with a heavy heart, made his way to the wharf.

Mary held her composure. "Be careful, Dan. I'll be waiting for you. We all will," she called after him, shyly patting her belly.

Freddie Mathews was a bright boy who recognized the seriousness of the situation. He had been only six years old when he had lost his uncle and grandfather but he remembered the horrid details and the grief it had caused everyone. Reading the worry on his mother's face and the apprehension in his father's movements, he was concerned about the well-being of his mother and the safety of his father. Nevertheless, he was filled with pride when Dan had called him into the woodshed and spoken to him privately. "You're the man of the house now, son. 'Tis all in your hands. You understand your mother's condition, so you have to take care of her and your little brother. The chores are your responsibility. I don't feel good about leaving, but it helps knowing that you are here to take care of things."

Freddie took the words to heart. He kept the wood-box and water barrel full. He kept the snow and ice away from the doors and pathways, and he fulfilled his mother's every request. Then, one night as the town slept, Mary woke Freddie with her cries. Freddie ran like the wind to the house of Mrs. Goodyear, the midwife, and banged on the porch door until a light appeared in an upstairs window. Before the sun rose, a tiny baby girl was nursing at his mother's breast.

"Your mother will need some good nourishment now that she's feeding two," Mrs. Goodyear had said to Freddie shortly after the baby was born. The comment lingered in Freddie's mind and haunted him like a curse from the fairies each time his mother became weak or when the baby cried excessively.

One morning after the baby cried all night, Mary handed Freddie a sealed envelope. "Take this to Mr. Briffett for me," she requested.

"What is it?" Freddie asked, taking the envelope, and looking dubiously into his mother's eyes.

"It's a letter for Mr. Briffett, explaining our predicament, and asking for a small advancement."

"But, what about Dad? He wouldn't want us to do that," he retorted, trying not to sound argumentative.

"Your father is not here, Freddie. He need not know."

"But Dad vowed never to ask Mr. Briffett for credit again."

"Now, you sound like your father, Freddie. I hope you are not like him—too proud for his own good. Besides, it's not your father asking, it's me."

Freddie entered Briffett's General Store and made his way to the back. Clutching the note tightly in his fist, he reluctantly approached the open office door. The man he had come to see was wearing a white shirt with silver sleeve garters that caused the sleeves to bunch above the elbows, and black suspenders that pulled a pair of pinstriped trousers high enough to be visible above the desk. Mr. Briffett was bent over a ledger, dabbing a pencil at the paper, like a woman hooking a mat. Freddie thought that his sharp features resembled the weasel his father had snared in the root cellar earlier in the winter, and he thought about the last time he had seen this man and about the confrontation between him and his father.

Freddie fully understood his mother's desperate position and wanted to honour her request, as he promised he would. He also knew that his father would not approve. Perplexed, Freddie stood frozen for a long time with the letter burning in his hands and his mind analyzing things far above his years. Finally, he turned abruptly and strutted toward the front door, tucking the envelope into his jacket pocket.

Once outside, he ran all the way back to his house and waited in the outside porch. When the baby cried and his mother went to her, Freddie dashed into the kitchen and removed the breechloader from its mount above the stove and grabbed the three cartridges from the dish on the mantle. Surely, his mother would understand why he didn't deliver the letter if he could bring home a saltwater bird or some other fresh game. He quietly closed the door and retreated from the house with gun in hand. Like a soldier on a mission, he took to the path along the shoreline and headed for the bird blind, scanning the water as he went. The warm sun of the past few days had caused part of the blind's walls to founder, and he spent valuable time fixing it up. Then, wishing that his father was with him, he crawled in and waited. It was a clear day with the wind pushing the ice toward the land. *Maybe it'll drive the birds close to shore.*

Freddie felt like a man, grasping the breechloader and astutely scanning the water and the sky, the way his father had taught him. As time passed, however, he felt the effects of being alone. The warmth of the sun and the sound of the tumbling waves were hypnotizing, and his imaginative mind wandered. He pictured a covey of black ducks flying straight for the blind, several of them tumbling from the sky, and he imagined himself presenting the delicious birds to his mother. He thought about his father, grandfather, and uncle, and he envisaged his father clambering over floating ice pans, lost, and searching for his ship.

Suddenly, the sound of flapping wings startled him from his reverie, and his heart leaped into his throat. A lone duck flew directly overhead. It was nearly out of range! He quickly jerked the gun to his shoulder, took rapid aim and squeezed the trigger. The blast was explosive, and the gun jumped from Freddie's grip. The hammer hooked his upper lip and ripped it. The hardwood stock kicked hard into his shoulder and sent him sprawling to the frozen ground.

"Bloody bastard," he muttered, choking back tears that had welled, remembering his father's warnings about holding the gun tightly. Feeling less like a man, he grabbed the gun, abandoned his post, and headed for home, blood dripping from his lip onto the white snow marking a trail of defeat. *Luck has abandoned this family.*

As he followed the path around the edge of Tug's Gulch, he instinctively searched the water and, much to his astonishment, spotted a large black duck bobbing near its rocky entrance. Freddie's keenness returned and his adrenalin surged. From the outcrop of rock on the north side of the gulch, he'd be able to get a clear shot. Forgetting about his throbbing lip, he dropped to his knees and cautiously crawled along the ice-encrusted rocks close to the water's edge.

This was a dangerous practice and he knew it. His father had warned him many times. Nevertheless, it was a chance he had to take. He slid along the slippery surface and dropped down between two rocks. Opening the breechloader, he took one of the remaining cartridges from his pocket and jammed it into the chamber. Cautiously, he peeked above the rocky barrier and searched the choppy water. The bird was nowhere to be seen. *Had it gone to wing while he was sneaking up? Most likely it dived.* Freddie pointed the gun in the general direction and pulled back the hammer, cocking the gun. He was ready. His heart pounded in his chest. His eyes darted from left to right. Suddenly, the big bird surfaced directly in front of him, well within range. Freddie squeezed the gun tight to his shoulder and held his breath. His finger tightened on the trigger. Visions of tender, juicy meat and steaming hot gravy filled his mind. It was a certain shot, he was sure of it. He told himself to shoot, but he did not. *Only three shells left. What if I miss? They must be kept in case of an emergency.*

With warm blood running over his chin, he kept his sights on the bird and watched as it swam out of range. Slowly, he lowered the gun from his shoulder and carefully disengaged it. He removed the cartridge and dropped it into his jacket pocket, the one holding the letter for Old Briffett—the letter he knew he would deliver. He knew that his father loved him more than anything and would understand his decision. Deep in his heart he knew that things would work out.

English 1000

Richard recognizes the man staring at him. *He has not aged well.* The man's once-thick black hair is now a mixture of grey and white, thin and wispy like maldow on a dying spruce tree. His once-vibrant pink skin is now pale and wrinkled, resembling a slab of rendered pork rind. His eyes, though, have maintained their dark piercing sharpness, and his jawline, its distinctive squareness.

To confirm, Richard checks the name plate at the foot of the bed and verifies it against the chart that he is holding. *Reginald Kirk Wellman, age 78.* It is a face he could never forget.

Richard is cast back many years—to being a teenager in a classroom in the province's only university. There was a lively buzz at the front of the room, similar to the buzz of the hospital ward where he is now standing. Students smoked cigarettes without fear of consequences, and a smoky haze hung in the air. The dull roar of the classroom stopped suddenly as a distinguished gentleman entered the room. He walked directly to the front of the classroom and placed his briefcase on a big desk. He turned to the chalkboard, picked up a stick of chalk, and wrote "R.K. WELLMAN" in scrawling handwriting. "Good morning students, I am Professor Wellman," he announced. "Welcome to English 1000."

Do I address him as Mr. Wellman or Professor Wellman? Without deciding, he speaks in a slow, clear voice, selecting his words carefully. "Good day, Mr. Wellman. I'm Doctor Macdonald. You have been assigned to my care. It seems, sir, that you have suffered an intracerebral hemorrhagic stroke. This is what has caused your paralysis and your slurred speech. Fortunately, Mr. Wellman, we have been able to minimize the trauma. I believe you have passed the critical point and I am not anticipating further incident ..."

The patient's gaze intensifies and Richard is again taken back—this time to his hometown and to the events leading up to English 1000 with Professor R.K. Wellman.

Richard sees himself lugging his suitcases to his father's wharf and lowering them aboard the boat. He was about to leave home for the first time, heading to university in the capital city. Most of the community's people were there to see him off, to say their farewells and wish him luck. His journey would take him first to St. Francis, 12 miles down the coast, where he would board a coastal boat for the three-hour trip along the coast to Safe Harbour, the place where the road met the water, connecting it to the rest of the province. Richard recalls the odd feeling of saying goodbye to the only people he ever knew. His mother was noticeably absent from the crowd—her tears had already been shed. No need to make a spectacle. Dandelions grew in abundance along the footpath to the wharf, raising their yellow heads and dancing in the wind. The grey-headed ones bowed submissively, dropping seeds so another generation could grow.

Steaming out the harbour, Richard looked back at the brightly painted homes of his hometown. They were shrouded in a silver haze. The sun penetrated the haze, magnifying the structures and causing them to appear larger than they really were. He focused on his own turquoise house, standing high and proud, like a monument to his childhood. The two upstairs window blinds were half drawn, each drooped, giving the little house a forlorn frown, a mood that matched his own.

Seagulls performed a ceremonial sendoff by circling the boat, squawking loudly. Richard wondered if they'd perform a similar ritual to welcome him home when he returned at Christmastime.

Rocky Gorge, long since resettled, was an isolated community on the rugged south coast of the island of Newfoundland. Its harbour was a mere gap chiselled into the rocky cliff, offering total protection from stormy winds and tumbling seas to 12 houses that stuck to the cliffs like puffins' nests. Each was supported on the front by starrigan sticks that ran all the way to the landwash. There was room for no more. Fishing stores, stages, and drying flakes were squeezed among the cluster. Vegetable gardens were located on a small plateau, high above the town—a hefty hike for even the most able-bodied.

Richard grins, remembering how his father surrendered to his mother's nagging and built a back porch on their house. He had resisted for years because the construction would mean blocking off the main path running around the community. He resolved the problem by building the porch with three doors—one giving entrance to the house and the other two, on opposite outside walls, allowing access to the outdoors. Those walking the path through the community in either direction simply entered one door, walked through the porch, and exited the other.

Life in Rocky Gorge was simple and honest. It revolved around hard work, family, friends, the church, and music. Richard had learned to love music from an early age. Each Saturday night the family kitchen would fill with anyone who could play an instrument or sing. His father was perhaps the best guitar player on the south coast and his mother had the voice of an angel. Richard learned to play his father's guitar and taught himself to play the old church pump organ. As a teen he was invited to play for Sunday church services, and he reluctantly accepted.

The little church was erected on the plateau among the vegetable gardens. A visiting minister held service a few times each year, but each Sunday the little church was always full to capacity, with Thomas Morris—one of the few in the community who could read and write— performing the service.

The one-room, all-grade schoolhouse was built adjacent to the church. The lone teacher (when one could be found) was responsible for the entire school curriculum, from Kindergarten to Grade 11. This was not a major issue because most pupils left school when they were old enough to help the family—with the household chores for the girls and fishing boats for the boys. Few ever made it into the higher grades. But Richard loved school, and he loved to read and to learn. The year he passed the Grade 9 government public examinations with honours the clergyman asked Richard to assist Mr. Morris by reading the scripture and meditations—and play the organ. Richard, though, respectfully declined the invitation. He was much too shy—playing music was one thing, but reading and speaking in public was something altogether different.

When Richard passed Grade 11 public examinations and became the first-ever student from Rocky Gorge to be admitted to the university in the city, everyone buzzed with excitement and pride. Finally, one of their own was going to break away from the fishery and make something of himself.

On the wharf in St. Francis, Richard hugged his father for the first time since he was a little boy, boarded the coastal steamer for Safe Harbour, and departed into the unknown. The sea was rough and the little steamer bobbed and rolled on the waves. For three hours Richard sat in the passenger lounge listening to other travellers chatting about things that were mostly unknown to him. He wondered if the queasiness in his belly was a result of seasickness or nervousness.

Finally, the sound of the engines eased into a purr and the ride became smoother. Passengers left the lounge and assembled on the deck. Richard followed. They were docking in Safe Harbour. His attention was immediately drawn to a wide gravel road that led from the wharf, meandered through the town and disappeared into the hills to the west. Multicoloured vehicles were parked near the docking platform and people were scurrying about. Other than pictures in his books, these were the first automobiles that Richard had ever seen. This was civilization.

"Where's the taxi that's going to St. John's?" Richard asked an elderly gentleman with a port wine birthmark on his left cheek.

"Right there, my son," the man replied, pointing to a dark green station wagon.

Richard paid his fare, loaded his luggage through the rear hatch, and boarded the crowded vehicle for a 12-hour, dusty, exhilarating ride to the city.

When he stepped from the taxi onto the university campus, he felt as if he had landed on another planet. Large buildings made of bricks towered into the sky. Some were adorned with fancy carvings, some were rectangular, others were asymmetrical, all had too many windows. He was amazed with the many flat, well-groomed grassy patches of land, all of which he would have loved to pick up and deposit in Rocky Gorge. Large concrete cauldrons like bark pots, with pretty flowers growing in them adorned the grassy areas. Heavy-topped trees, groomed and evenly spaced, provided shelter for benches. People were everywhere. Some were bunched together, while others were scurrying like ants along the many cement paths that connected the buildings.

Richard pulled an envelope from his inside jacket pocket and checked the name on an official university document against a brass plaque above the front door of a dormitory building. The two matched. He entered the grandiose structure with trepidation. After walking the length of a long corridor, he saw a directory that told him that room 413 was on the fourth floor.

He mucked his heavy suitcases up the steep stairs. The door to room 413 was ajar. Richard entered with apprehension. It was how he imagined a prison cell: cold concrete walls, grey linoleum tiles on the floor. Very little light made its way through a single, dirty window, and the smell of insecticide permeated the air. Two single beds ran parallel to each other with barely enough room to rest a suitcase between them. Someone had carved into the cork bulletin board above one of the beds, *procrastination is the thief of time*. Richard remembered his father saying over and over, *time waits for no man*. He reasoned that it was the same quote, only stated in a more sophisticated way. Exhausted from the long trip, Richard curled up on one of the beds and fell asleep. He dreamed about Rocky Gorge and his cozy upstairs bedroom with its window overlooking the water.

He was awakened by the sound of voices in the corridor. When he stepped from his room, he noticed that most of the doors were open and boys, in various stages of undress, were dashing to and from the washrooms. Some were standing about, engaged in conversation. It seemed as if all were known to each other.

"Where are you from?" asked a boy with hair that hung all the way to his shoulders.

"Rocky Gorge."

"Where's that?"

"South Coast. How about you? Where are you from?"

"Cow Head."

"Where's that?"

"Northern Peninsula."

Richard was soon mingling among the crowd, boys from all across the island and a few from the mainland. All were already paired with roommates—most of their own choosing, friends from the same town or classmates from the same school.

"Who's your roommate?" someone asked.

"I don't know. Don't have one yet," Richard replied.

Because Richard had not requested a roommate, one was to be chosen for him by the Housing Office. He was anxious to learn who it would be.

He did not have to wait long. That evening, when he returned from the evening meal at the dining hall, he found his room door open. A dark-skinned figure was sitting on a bulging suitcase, strumming a guitar.

"Are you Richard?" the young man asked, flashing a beaming white smile.

"Yes, I am."

"I'm Tunda, your roommate," he said, extending his hand.

Receiving the hand, Richard noticed that Tunda's palms were as white as his own, and that his grip was soft and warm. It was the first non-white person that Richard had ever seen, other than in his Grade 4 geography book.

"Where are you from?" Richard asked.

"I come from 'the giant of Africa.' From Nigeria," Tunda replied. He then played and sang a Nigerian folk song with such emotion that in spite of not understanding the words, Richard felt the sentiment of the lyrics. He watched, in fascination, at the way that Tunda tweaked at the strings with the fingertips of his right hand.

"You have a unique way of picking," he commented.

"Do you play the guitar?" Tunda asked.

"A little, but not like you."

"Come, I teach you how I play."

Richard took the guitar and strummed a chord, and Tunda showed him how to create the same sound by plucking individual strings. Richard, in turn, showed Tunda how to run chords together, and the two distinctive roommates played and talked into the early morning hours.

The following morning Tunda and Richard ate breakfast together at the main dining hall of the dormitory complex. The two discussed different foods from their respective homelands. Richard bragged about salt fish with scrunchions, pork toutons, and partridgeberry tarts; Tunda went on about pounded yams, garri, and egusi soup.

After breakfast, Tunda, a third-year student, gave Richard a thorough guided tour of the entire campus. Richard was particularly intrigued with a system of tunnels that connected the dormitories to all of the academic buildings. The people of Rocky Gorge would not believe this.

The next morning Richard descended into these tunnels and made his way to his first class—English 1000.

Professor Wellman opened his briefcase, withdrew a plain brown paper bag, and shook it in the air as if its purpose was to frighten away blue-arsed flies from a screen door.

"In this bag I have placed small pieces of paper on which I have written one word. Each student is to draw from the bag and speak for three minutes on the word written on the paper."

Then, he produced a plain manila file folder and withdrew a single sheet of paper. "And here I have a class list. From it I will randomly select the order in with each of you will speak." He ran his finger down the paper, halting halfway. "Richard Macdonald," he called.

Richard's heart leaped into his throat and his face flushed. He sank into his seat, hoping that he could disappear or that the professor would move to another name.

"Mr. Macdonald, please identify yourself," the professor persisted, searching the classroom with his dark eyes.

Richard raised his hand slowly and sheepishly, like a schoolboy caught in a lie.

"Very well, Mr. Macdonald, please come forward."

Richard's heart thumped in his chest, and he felt an urge to urinate. He left his seat and walked to the front of the classroom. His ears were ringing, his legs weak and rubbery.

Professor Wellman held out the bag in front of Richard and gave it another shake.

Richard hesitated. The professor shook the bag again and nudged it forward. With a trembling hand, Richard reached into the bag. He was reminded of the time the minister asked him to draw the winning ticket for a quilt at the Women's Church Social. He withdrew a folded paper and handed it to the professor, expecting him to open it to announce that someone had won a prize.

Professor Wellman raised his hand with open palm, declining the offer. "No, Mr. Macdonald, you open it and please disclose the topic you have chosen."

Richard unfolded the paper. *PIGS*.

"It says 'pigs,' sir," Richard said, barely audible.

"I'm sorry. Please speak up, Mr. Macdonald."

"Pigs, sir. It says pigs."

"Very well, please introduce yourself, tell the class where you are from, and speak for three minutes on the topic you have selected."

Richard was now trembling. He looked around the room; all eyes were staring at him. His instinct was to bolt from the room—escape—back to Rocky Gorge, back to his safe haven. He opened his mouth to speak, to introduce himself, but his mouth was powder-dry, and the words would not come.

Finally, he licked his lips, swallowed a lump in his throat, and found his voice. "My name is Richard Macdonald, and I come from Rocky Gorge." Then he stopped. *Pigs ... pigs. No one kept pigs in Rocky Gorge. What can I say about pigs?* There was an awkward silence, his mind raced like the gears of father's old outboard motor the time he twisted off the shaft. He knew nothing about pigs. *Hens ... Why didn't I pick hens? Everyone kept hens. I know everything about hens ... eggs ... and roosters too.*

"I'm afraid I don't know much about pigs, sir, except ... the story of the *Three Little Pigs*."

"Very well, then, relate to the class the story of the *Three Little Pigs*," the professor replied.

Richard furrowed his forehead and looked at the professor in disbelief. This is not what he was expecting from *the* institution of higher learning. He dropped his head, focused on the floor, took a deep breath and, in his thick accent, began, "Once upon a time ..."

Richard realized that Tunda spoke English with a pronounced accent, but was unaware that his own was equally distinct. Most Newfoundlanders, city and rural alike, spoke in the accents of their European ancestry. The *h* sound was often added before a vowel where it was not needed and frequently dropped when it was required.

The *th* sound, as well as the ending consonant sounds, were frequently dropped.

Richard's Rocky Gorge accent was filled with inflections and intonations from the language of the old country that had been preserved because of isolation. Certain words and sayings had become bastardized over time and were nowhere to be found in any dictionary. To add to its distinctiveness, the residents of Rocky Gorge had developed a method of speaking in which they exhaled words quickly without exercising the physical articulators. This gave their speech a musical quality but made it difficult to understand for those unfamiliar with it.

At one point, several pretty girls in the front row snickered. Richard chuckled also, not because he saw humour in the situation but to hide his mortification.

"Thank you very much, Mr. Macdonald," Professor Wellman said politely when Richard had finished.

Richard returned to his seat feeling how he imagined Herman Mullins, a timid boy, must had felt the time he soiled his clothes after being asked to recite the Apostles' Creed during his Confirmation but was unable to do so. Richard struggled to stay focused while the other students took their turn and made their speeches.

Some speeches were entertaining, others were funny, and a few received applause from the class. All, he felt, had performed better than he had. *Maybe if I had not gone first, I would have made less of a fool of myself.*

At the end of the class, Professor Wellman circulated a list of required readings for the course—periodicals that were to be found in the reserve section of the library, as well as several expensive books to be purchased from the on-campus bookstore. In addition, the professor assigned a research paper—an in-depth biography on a prolific 19th-century writer. Richard perked up. Charles Dickens immediately came to his mind. He had been introduced to Dickens in high school and had read most of his works. A paper on Dickens would be easy and interesting. However, his excitement was dashed when the professor informed them that the paper was to be presented in a 30-minute oral presentation.

Richard felt defeated. He could not imagine speaking again in front of these people, certainly not for 30 minutes. His head pounded as he left the classroom. He descended into the poorly lit tunnels and retreated to his dormitory room. He had other classes on his schedule for that day, but he attended neither. Alone in his room, he reasoned that he had made a huge mistake by leaving Rocky Gorge. He was a strange fish swimming in strange water. Everything was so different, he could never adjust, never fit in. He decided that he was going home to the people he knew and loved, to a way of life he appreciated and understood.

That evening Tunda found Richard sobbing into his pillow. "My roommate not happy?"

"I made a fool of myself, Tunda. I'm quitting. I'm going home."

"That premature decision, my friend. You need to fight your emotions and reason things out."

"But I don't belong here, Tunda. I'm not like the other students. I'm different."

Tunda sat beside Richard and placed a hand on his roommate's shoulder, and spoke softly. "Richard, look at your roommate. You look into my face—do you see the colour of my skin? I know the meaning of being different, but I never quit. Before I came to this country, my grandfather, the most senior and wisest man in our community, tell me that different is good. He tell me to never think myself inferior to another and never to think another inferior to me. I follow my grandfather's words on my journey. All people are different, my friend, because of where we come from, but no one is better than another. Our differences only distinguish who we are; we must embrace our differences and respect those who are different from us."

Tunda's words were sincere and inspirational, but Richard had made up his mind. He had convinced himself that he had been overly ambitious, that he had set his goals too high. It was a mistake to think that there was a future for him outside Rocky Gorge. He was going home.

That night, sleep did not come easy. Richard twisted and turned until the early morning hours. When he finally did drift off, he dreamed that he was back in Rocky Gorge in his little house on the cliff. A storm was raging and rain was beating against the kitchen window. His father was asleep on the daybed; Luke, the cat, was curled up at his feet. His mother was fussing around the kitchen with her apron strings flowing freely. Heat radiating from the woodstove filled the small space, and the smell of homemade bread permeated the air. He was sitting at the kitchen table reading a book. He was cozy, content, and secure.

In the morning he slept late. He did not hear Tunda get up and leave for his classes. Richard revisited the events of the previous day and the decision he had made. There was no dilemma. He was as content as he had been in his dream and proceeded to repack his suitcase with the few things he had already sorted in his tiny closet. At noon, he realized that he had not eaten since the previous morning, so he headed to the dining hall. After getting his meal card punched and making his way through the food line, he was met with a long line of students standing around, holding their full food trays, waiting for a vacant seat. Several complained that the dining area was too small and that additional space needed to be added. Picking a roll from his tray and biting into it, Richard scanned the crowded room. He spotted Tunda sitting alone at a small round table with three empty chairs. His roommate flashed his shiny smile as Richard approached the table.

"See," Tunda said, kicking out one of the empty chairs. "There are some advantages to being different. I have chair for my friend to sit."

Richard rested his food tray on the table, sat down, and looked hard at his friend. Nodding to the empty chairs, he asked, "Does it bother you, Tunda?"

Tunda slowly wiped his mouth with a napkin before speaking. "Sometimes I feel sad, but I understand that ignorance is innocent. I know who I am, and I am proud of where I come from—that is all that matters."

Richard concentrated on the food before him and was silent, processing Tunda's words. "Tunda, my father would like you," he said eventually. "He would say that you are your own man. He would say that you have inner strength. It would please him very much if I were more like you."

"I think you very much like me, Richard."

Richard slowly looked around the dining room and

smiled. "I think I am too—no—I bloody well know I am."

The two roommates ate lunch together. No one joined them.

With Tunda's help, Richard learned to use the university library, and completed his research paper on Charles Dickens in less than a week. When it was complete, he rehearsed it each night, first in front of a mirror, then in front of Tunda.

"You get better each time," Tunda said encouragingly.

Three days before the presentation, Richard lost his appetite, and the smell of the dining-hall food nauseated him.

On the day of the presentation, a thousand seagulls fluttered in his stomach. Tunda accompanied Richard to his classroom and waited outside the door until they spotted Professor Wellman coming down the corridor. Richard took a deep breath, high-fived his roommate, and walked into the room.

When his name was called, Richard walked to the podium with legs of rubber, his hands quivering like a flatfish pinned to the ocean bottom with a fish prong. This time he was not the first one to present. More than half the class had gone before him on previous days. He took comfort, and gained confidence, in knowing his topic well and in believing that his paper was as good or better prepared than many he had heard.

"I have chosen Charles Dickens as the topic of my presentation," Richard said. Then, through parched lips and in a crackling voice, he dropped his eyes to his paper and read. His objective was to get the job done, not to be dramatic.

When he was finished, there were no questions from the class as there had been for other students—no comment from Professor Wellman. He returned to his seat, feeling the weight of a thousand punt loads of fish lifted from his shoulders. It was the first of many presentations Richard was to make throughout his long university career and since.

Richard addresses his patient. "It is now a matter of monitoring your progress over the next while, and then concentrating on rehabilitation to help you recover as much function as possible and prevent future strokes. I will be arranging physical and occupational therapy to help you recover from the weakness and the paralysis. And, at the same time, I will order speech therapy to help with the post-stroke language problems and cognitive therapy to help with any issues like memory." The irony of his comments was not lost on Richard.

"Unfortunately, Mr. Wellman, prognosis is uncertain. The success rate and the recovery time differ from patient to patient. Much of it depends on you. We must stay optimistic and hope for the best. Do you understand what I am saying, Mr. Wellman?"

Professor Wellman slowly closes his dark eyes and nods his head a few times. Richard recalls the comments written on his Dickens research paper: *Well researched, superbly written. Oral presentation weak; generally poor elocution; needs to show more confidence.* He smiles, wondering if it is possible that the professor also recognizes him. He feels an urge to confess that he had once been his student, that he was the shy boy from Rocky Gorge, the one with the funny accent. Then he thinks about Tunda and wonders what became of him. He thinks about the words of Tunda's grandfather. He says nothing.

In Pursuit

Alexander sniffed the air as he boarded the train. *Am I supposed to feel something?* This was the land of his birth—the place where he lost his baby teeth and his virginity. Where he went to school, where he made enemies and lost friends. His ancestors are buried in this ground. His parents were getting old and would likely need him. But Alexander could only think escape—escape the social bickering, the monotony, the poverty. *The city will bring excitement and adventure. The city will make me rich.*

Within a week of arriving in the big city, Alexander abandoned his faded, dated wardrobe and worked his way into the urban fabric. He trained his palate to accept grease-laden food, his nostrils to tolerate the smell of chlorinated water, and his ears to absorb noisy music. He worked hard to rid himself of his thick accent which he thinks flat and inferior. But there was an advantage to the brogue. Some women, assuming it to be from parts more exotic, found it sexy. It helped him get laid—often enough to put a bump on the perfect body of the beautiful girl who worked in the tall glass building. She was afraid to have a child—lines would mark her belly and her perky breasts would sag. Alexander was afraid also—his career was rapidly advancing. He did not have the time to become a parent.

When twin girls were born, however, paternal instincts surfaced. Each were as proud as any parent could be.

It was not the perfect family, but Mom was nurturing and Alexander was the great provider. Remembering his own childhood, Alexander thinks, *my children will not know poverty.*

The clock rings—Saturday morning, 6 a.m.

"Okay children, outta bed, it's our big day."

"It's too early for the park."

"Time is money ... important meeting at two."

"But you don't work on Saturdays, Daddy."

"Today I do, so let's get moving."

"Will other kids be there?"

"How am I to know? I've never been to a park."

"Is Mommy going?"

"No."

"Why not?"

"Says it's my turn."

Alexander tightens his grip on the skipping girls as they make their way through the city streets. The children sing and are happy. They have never seen the streets at this early hour. They swing on their father's arm and strain to investigate the refuse left after a Friday night of adult merriment. Empty coffee cups whirl in the wind, French fry plates flap flirtatiously, pop cans spill sticky remains. There are many strange things that the children have not seen before.

"What's the white thing, Daddy?"

"Nothing!"

"But it looks like a ...!"

"Don't touch that!"

Alexander increases his pace and tugs hard. The youngsters whimper and protest.

"The city streets are unsafe. We must hurry." Alexander suddenly stiffens like a startled snake. A fresh fifty-dollar bill is lying on the littered pavement. It is overwhelmingly inviting, and Alexander stretches an arm and strains to retrieve it.

"Look out, Daddy!"

Alexander jumps back as a city bus swerves to avoid

him. He is shaken and slackens his hold on his little girls. They retreat to the sidewalk and stand in silence. Alexander loses sight of the money. He shields his eyes and searches the street. Then, he spots the precious paper fluttering in the air like an injured bird, being sucked along in the vacuum of the bus. Like a crisp autumn leaf, it settles on the pavement, at the mouth of a side street—a goal within reach, a risk worth taking.

Alexander searches his surroundings and spots a city bench.

"Sit here, children, until I return!"

He leaves the children and runs along the sidewalk. Carefully, he negotiates the traffic and works his way closer to his goal. He is near enough to feel victory when a competing draft draws the bill into the side street and hurls it into the busy avenue opposite. Alexander gives chase. He dashes through the side street, into the busy avenue. He spots the red bill near the middle of the avenue; whizzing traffic impedes his pursuit. Then, a speeding vehicle sends the flimsy paper fluttering into flight, high above the traffic.

A man dressed in an executive suit stands at a newsstand reading a morning paper. The bill sweeps skyward, directly in front of the man and softly settles at his feet. He slightly furrows his brow, stoops slowly, and, with forefinger and thumb, gingerly picks up the surrendering note. He smiles at his good luck and pockets his find.

"Stop!" shouts a frantic Alexander.

"Yes?"

"You have my money."

"Oh, you lost it?"

"Well, I've been chasing it."

"And I have found it."

The dialogue is sustained and sometimes passionate. The man in the suit is sympathetic and Alexander spots a weakness. The two deliberate at a nearby coffee shop where Alexander supplies coffee and makes an offer. The man accepts a small reward, and Alexander proudly pockets his prize.

He whistles cheerfully as he retraces his route to the city bench. Much to his amazement, the children are not to be seen. They have moved on to play with the strange things in the street.

The Christmas Card

Seventy-five-year-old John James Feltham sits in his modest apartment in an eastern suburb on the outskirts of Toronto watching two cats play on the newly paved parking lot outside his window. The surrounding buildings cast ominous shadows and the wind funnels through the narrow alleyways, blowing litter about. For the best part of an hour, he has been enjoying the antics of the two young felines as they chase a rolling pop can and attack an empty cigarette package. He wonders if they are strays or if they belong to someone living in his building.

"Do you think cats care about where they live?" he asks his wife, Maggie.

"I think cats are like people—it depends on what they're used to. Wild cats don't make good pets, while you don't take a house cat and drive it outdoors," she answers confidently.

Maggie is busy preparing a Christmas fruitcake and keeps her attention on the task at hand. The smell of mixed fruit, ginger, and nutmeg fills the tiny living space, mixing with the stale marijuana that creeps into the apartment from the corridor.

She lifts a cast iron baking pot from a cupboard beneath the sink. "I'm some glad I brought this one with me," she mumbles, barely loud enough for her husband to hear.

"Yes, because you can't buy them like that anymore, and if you could, we'll never live long enough to break it in," John James remarks.

The baking pot was one of the few cooking utensils that she had taken from her kitchen in Shoal Bay when they were resettled. It had been in Maggie's family for a long time—handed down from her great-grandmother, who had gotten it as a wedding gift when she was still living in the old country. Most of the other pots, pans, and dishes she had left in the house, just in case they returned some summer for a week or two. Or perhaps their son, Edward, might take his children there sometime, to show them where their father had grown up. The government had allowed the residents of Shoal Bay to keep their houses as summer homes or a station from which to fish—but all subsidies were to be discontinued. Most of the residents were adamant that they would not let the place die and kept their homes livable, vowing to return whenever they could. All except Harvey Williams. Harvey vowed that Shoal Bay was dead, and he would not allow his house to become victim to the elements or be ravaged by a bunch of trophy-seeking hoodlums. He emptied the house of everything, including the kitchen cupboards, soaked it in gasoline, and set it ablaze.

The move to Toronto from Shoal Bay was traumatizing for Maggie. Until then the farthest she had travelled was a four-hour ferry ride to Seal Lake, the closest town that had shops, a hospital, and a few government offices.

The move was equally difficult for John James. *A fish out of water* is cliché, but there is no analogy more appropriate. He had once been to St. John's on a fishing schooner to offload salt cod, and once to Halifax on a coastal trader to pick up a load of lumber. Other than that, his entire life was spent in Shoal Bay, the place he will always call home. There had been little reason to travel anywhere else. For centuries, the people of the isolated outport had set deep roots, harvesting a living from the sea. The work was dangerous and demanding; money was scarce and times were often hard, but there was always food on the table, and the way of life was simple and honest.

Change came when the fish stocks dwindled and a government-imposed moratorium shut down the cod fishery—the mainstay of survival. Veteran fishermen were forced to abandoned the only jobs they knew and encouraged to learn new and unfamiliar trades. Those who were young and brave enough to retrain found work in towns, cities, and construction sites all over the country. In the beginning they left their families at home and commuted. Some came home on weekends, others during off-shifts and on holidays. Eventually, though, the residents of the town realized the advantages of living in the place where they worked and more and more of them relocated their families. Maggie and John James's only son, Edward, and his family were among them.

As the population of Rocky Shoal dropped, so did government services. The school became the first victim. Students as young as 13 were given bursaries and sent to schools in bigger communities, away from home. The ferry service was cut back to three runs per week, and the government wharf deteriorated, with no plans to repair it. When the medical clinic was reduced to one nurse and ambulatory ferry service scaled back to emergency cases only, some of the younger folks requested that government initiate its resettlement policy. Government, seeing it as a cost-saving measure, readily agreed—as long as the majority of the community consented. John James and his best friend, Tommy, vowed that they were going nowhere, and protested long and hard.

The two cats scamper off when the mailman cuts across the parking lot.

"Mailman is here, Mag," John James announces.

Maggie finishes pouring the cake mixture into the baking pot and places it in the oven. Without speaking, she cleans her hands in her apron and goes to check the mailbox. The mailroom was on the ground floor, down the stairwell at the end of a long narrow hallway. It was a short distance, but it was a journey that always made her feel uneasy.

She returns, holding a single envelope that she hands to John James. "It's addressed to you."

John James looks puzzled. "Me? Sure, the pension cheques came last week."

"'Tis personal mail. Done out in handwriting. Looks like a Christmas card."

John James receives the envelope like one reaching for a newborn baby. He holds it in his huge calloused hands for a long time, studying it. Finally, he takes a pocketknife from his trousers pocket and gingerly slits along the crease at the top. He carefully pulls a card from the envelope and holds it out like an open hymn book. Maggie leans over his shoulder, admiring the picture on the front of the card.

"Lovely!" she says.

It's a scene of a little country church on a moonlit night. Candles burning in the church windows, large fluffy snowflakes falling. The lights of a little village are visible in the background. People are making their way over a snowy path to the church. Immediately, John James thinks of the last Christmas in Shoal Bay. To Christmas Eve, and attending midnight service, the same as he had done as long as he could remember. The church was full with familiar, friendly, smiling faces. The pump organ bellowed and familiar carols reverberated off the walls. Evelyn Warren's face was blood-red and the veins in her neck bulged as she sang slightly off-key, in a scratchy voice. John James recalls walking home after the service, the smell of wood smoke lingering in the frigid air, the crunch of footsteps in the frosty snow singing out. The smell of the bird cooking in the oven welcomes him home as he enters the porch, and he knows he will rob the neck and have a shot of rum before he goes to bed. He thinks about the 12 days of celebrations that will follow, with mummers in weird disguises, playing lively accordion music, tapping out the tunes on the kitchen floor. He reminisces about the times in the Fisherman's Hall, where men, women, and children indulge in boilers of homemade soup and dance square sets until after bedtime. He remembers the sound of shotgun blasts echoing through the harbour on New Year's Eve, welcoming in the New Year. He wonders how they celebrate Christmas here in Toronto. *God help the person who fires off a gun here on New Year's Eve.*

John James licks his thumb and flicks open the card. A verse in the shape of a bell adorns one side of the card. A brief handwritten note is written on the other. He recognizes only the words *Merry Christmas.*

"Here, see what dis says," he asks, handing the card to Maggie.

Maggie takes the card and is silent for a long time. Finally, she says, "Lovely verse."

"Never mind the verse, who's it from?"

"Tommy," she answers.

"Tommy," he repeats in a whisper. "Where's he at?"

"He says he finally made up his mind and went to St. John's—wants to be close to the hospitals."

"St. John's ... I knew dat's where he'd end up," John James muttered.

Again, John James drifts back to Shoal Bay. He and Tommy were leaning over the back fence that separates their properties and talking about the resettlement vote.

"So, how do you think the vote will go? Think they'll get the 90 per cent?"

"I don't know what to think, Tommy, boy, other than it got this town tore apart. Families are not speakin' to one another over it. People don't know what to do."

"Well, I knows what to do and how I'll be votin'. I'm too old to be pullin' up roots, and besides, I have nowhere to go," Tommy declared.

"But, we gotta think about the young ones, Tommy. There's nothing left here for them, and soon there will be nothing left for any of us."

"You're not turnin' soft are ya, John James Feltham?"

"I know I said at first that I'd never leave, but the more I listen to the other side of things, there's an awful lot to think about."

"That's a fact, but I already got me cemetery plot paid fer, and I can't imagine not being buried next to Sarah."

"I s'pose they can always bring ya back to bury ya, Tommy."

"Yes, but whose gonna look after the cemetery? Won't take the alder bushes long to take over."

"Sometimes I think that it doesn't matter much. We

only go back to nature. Half the plots up at the cemetery are full of artificial flowers, anyway. Alders are more natural than plastic flowers."

When the time came, though, it was a different matter. The government propaganda and pressure from the rest of the community were too much. The two old friends reluctantly voted with the majority.

John James and Maggie's choice was relatively obvious. They moved upalong, to Toronto, to be close to their only son, Edward, and their grandchildren. Tommy's decision was more difficult. He was alone in the world, no family to follow and no desire to live anywhere else. He was the last person to leave Rocky Shoal, not because of stubbornness but because he simply had nowhere to go.

"St. John's ... well ... well," John James mutters. "Tommy living in St. John's and me on the mainland. What a turn of events. I would never have thought it."

Tommy and John James were only two months apart in age. As boys, they played together, although boyhood was short-lived in Shoal Bay in those days. Both boys took to the fishing boat with their fathers at age 12 and worked to contribute to the family income. After a few years, when they became old enough to branch out on their own, they became partners and fished in the same boat until old age and a modest government cheque encouraged them to stay ashore.

Tommy used to heave back in the punt, with his hand on the tiller, his leg cocked over the gunwale, and a mischievous gleam in his eye. John James's mouth waters as he recalls allowing the skiff to drift freely after pulling the traps, selecting a fresh codfish from the day's catch, and stewing it up on the after-thwart, with sea water and sweet onions. He hears the screams of seagulls fighting over the few scraps thrown overboard, and he feels a warm salty breeze on his face and sees the sun dancing on the waves.

John James chuckles about the time Tommy overreached while retrieving the mooring buoy and fell into the icy water, and how John James hooked a gaff into Tommy's jacket collar and dragged him into the punt, flipping and flopping, like an oversize salmon retrieved from the cod-trap leader.

He shivers, remembering getting stranded on the icefield off Eastern Head while hunting seals. It had started off as a calm, sunny spring day, but a sudden change of wind pushed the pack ice offshore, leaving open water between the men and the land. The temperature had plummeted and the air became laden with wet snow. In a matter of minutes, the pair lost sight of the land and were hopelessly stranded. Maggie sounded the alarm when darkness set in and her husband and Tommy had not returned. The town's people combed the shoreline, firing off guns and lighting fires—there was little else to do. Everyone knew the dangers of the pack ice and feared the outcome of being stranded on it. Maggie was frantic with worry and walked the floor for the entire night, wringing her hands and whimpering. They were adrift for over 24 hours on a floating icefield, bobbing in the frigid and unforgiving North Atlantic. The two friends had never felt closer—closer even than when Sarah had died. They clung to each other to stay warm, stared death in the face, and cried in each other's arms. They offered reassurance when one or the other became discouraged. They sang hymns and they prayed for a miracle. Just as all hope was fading and their bodies nearly drained of life, two bird hunters from Backside Cove, a neighbouring community, spotted the lost men and came to the rescue.

John James beams with pride when he remembers Albert Loder from up the shore wrongly accusing him of hauling his lobster traps and came into town, fired up with liquor, looking for trouble. The much bigger man caught up with him on the steps of the General Store and was about to lay a beating on him when Tommy showed up and dropped Albert with a single punch.

Thinking back even further, John James remembers the two young buckos traipsing over the snowy path to Backside Cove, on their way to attend a time in the parish hall. As if it were yesterday, he can see Maggie and Sarah sitting on a bench next to the potbelly stove. He smiles when he recollects Tommy saying, "I want the one on the left."

Tommy and Sarah were the first to marry—four years before Maggie and John James. John James pictures himself at their wedding, drinking moonshine in the woodshed before the ceremony, standing in church as his friend's best man, and dancing Maggie around the floor of the schoolhouse until the early hours of the morning.

He will never forget how Tommy had sunk into himself when he lost Sarah and child during childbirth— how afterwards, he refused to move back into an empty house, and lived with Maggie and him for two whole months. They'd hear Tommy crying in the middle of the night; he nearly pined away from not eating.

The last time John James saw Rocky Shoal, he and Maggie were standing on the deck of the ferry as it pulled away from the dock. Maggie was waving goodbye to those friends who had not yet left and were gathered on the wharf. John James searched the crowd, looking for Tommy, but he was nowhere to be seen. As the ferry pulled farther into the harbour, their house came into view and Maggie pointed to it. The plywood sheeting over the windows made it look like a dead friend. Maggie started to cry.

A movement outside the apartment window catches John James's attention. One of the cats has returned. It is wandering around the parking lot, meowing, calling to the other cat. John James scans the parking lot, looking for the other cat, but it is nowhere to be seen.

"I s'pose I'll never see Tommy again," he says to Maggie.

Maggie pulled down the oven door, checked her cake, and pretended not to hear.

John James looks down at his Christmas card. A tear rolls down his weathered face and falls upon the little church. He had never before received a Christmas card.

The Lighthouse Keeper and the Doctor

Victor Manuel had been the lighthouse keeper on Green Island for his entire adult life. He had seen it many times before at this time of the year—an intense storm system, formed in the warm climates to the south, was slamming the northeast coast of Newfoundland. For the past 10 days, gale-force winds had created hazardous conditions that brought sea traffic to a halt and stranded Victor on the island. He had been due to change shifts four days earlier, but the swelling seas and breaking shoals made passage into the harbour impossible, and it prevented Raymond House, the second lighthouse keeper, from leaving the shore. When a lighthouse keeper took up post on Green Island, he was never certain when he'd be relieved of his duties.

Victor busied himself with the daily chores of running a lighthouse, the most important of which was keeping the beacon light flashing, guiding the sea traffic, and warning about breakers lurking beneath the surface. Today he was extra vigilant, frequently scanning the distant horizon and searching the shoreline for anything out of the ordinary. There was always the possibility that some vessel from unknown parts, ignorant to the fact that the harbour's entrance was too dangerous to navigate in a storm, might come seeking shelter. And there was always the chance that some bird hunter on the shore could get caught by a rogue wave and be washed from the cliffs. He had to be always ready to sound the alarm.

Today, though, the only traffic was that of larger ocean-going ships that kept well offshore in the shipping lanes. Nevertheless, Victor's trained eye followed each one until it disappeared from sight.

In the mid-afternoon he observed dark, threatening clouds festering in the east when a vessel appeared in his spyglass far to the south. Victor noted that the ship was steaming directly toward Green Island.

"Hope she's not expecting to enter the harbour," Victor said aloud, a habit he developed a long time ago to deal with the loneliness of a lighthouse keeper's life.

As the ship got closer, he recognized it as the SS *Glencoe,* a coastal steamer—the proverbial link to the outside world. Victor relaxed. He knew the vessel was making her final run of the season northward to Labrador, and he knew that Captain Jacob was familiar with the coast, enough not to attempt to enter the harbour in this wind.

He knew exactly what would happen. The big ship would seek shelter in the tickle behind the island and heave to. A small tender would be launched, mail and small packages would be loaded aboard and brought to Green Island for the lighthouse keeper to deliver when the wind abated. It was not a requirement of a lighthouse keeper's duties, but it was a service they had been providing for many years. It was the least they could do. The people of Sound Harbour waited long enough for supplies and communication with the outside world. The larger freight would be left aboard until the return trip, when hopefully the weather would be more civil and the ship able to enter the harbour.

The steamer's whistle sounded as it approached, and Victor responded with two quick blasts of the lighthouse horn. Communication had been established. Exactly as predicted, the ship sought the shelter of the island and anchored in the tickle. Several deckhands appeared on deck and skilfully launched a small tender into the swelling sea. Two of them hopped aboard the small heaving boat with the agility of logrollers. Victor focused his spyglass and watched as three canvas mailbags were thrown into the tender. Then, surprisingly, he noticed a large fancy-looking suitcase being lowered into the smaller boat. Captain William Jacob appeared on deck and walked to where the tender was tied. He was followed by a smaller man wearing a tweed fedora, black wool raglan, and black rubber galoshes. Victor focused on the second man but did not recognize him. *One thing for sure, he's certainly not from around here.*

A rope ladder was lowered over the side of the steamer into the tender, and Captain Jacob climbed down. He helped the stranger into the smaller boat and ushered him to the stern, in the shelter of the little engine house. The captain cupped his hands over his mouth and shouted orders to a crewmember on the deck of the steamer and the ladder was retrieved, the lines let go, and the small boat headed toward Green Island.

"Funny, why is Captain Jacob bringing a stranger to the island? I wonder who he is. There's no election, so 'tis not a politician," Victor said aloud.

There was only one place on the island to land a boat and it was no easy task when the sea was swelling. Victor hurried to prepare the slipway. The island ascended from the sea like a stone fortress with high granite cliffs all around. On the south side, a narrow rocky gorge cut into the cliffs and sloped into the sea, at the end of which was a small rocky beach. There, a slipway made of round sticks was hinged into the rocks just above high-water mark. It was lifted and lowered, using a block-and-tackle pulley system whenever a boat needed to land. Victor lowered the slipway into the water as the tender approached, rising and falling on the huge swells. One of the deckhands threw the painter; Victor caught it and pulled the boat in to the end stick of the slipway. The same deckhand jumped to the beach, and he and Victor vigorously hauled the craft farther over the round sticks until only its stern remained in the water.

Captain Jacob hopped upon the gunwale, leaped to the beach and, in a flash, was standing in front of Victor, extending a huge gloved hand. "Good to see ya, Victor. How have you been?"

"Better than the weather," Victor replied, receiving the captain's hand.

"I brought the mail ashore for you to drop off."

"That I see, and what else can I do for you?" he asked, shifting his gaze to the stranger who was being assisted out of the boat by the two deckhands.

"I got your new doctor here. Don't want to lug him all the way to Labrador and back. I was wondering if you can put him up until the wind breaks?"

Victor responded with a grin. "Well, you didn't bring

him and his luggage ashore expectin' me to turn him away now did you?"

Captain Jacob let out a hearty laugh and patted Victor on the back. "I knew I could count on you, Victor." Then, he turned to the doctor who was awkwardly creeping his way over the beach rocks. "Victor, I'd like you to meet Doctor Seward."

A fine kid glove and a scruffy woollen mitten were removed, and the doctor and the lighthouse keeper dubiously and awkwardly shook hands. One was soft and refined, the other rigid and coarse. The whole exercise looked more like two children rehearsing for a school concert than it did an official salutation. As the two exchanged pleasantries, each man was required to exercise linguistic interpretative skills: the well-educated doctor spoke formally and eloquently in a thick and sophisticated brogue; the self-taught lighthouse keeper spoke with lyrical quickness, in a blunt and flat accent.

"I beg your pardon?" questioned the doctor.

"What was that you said?" Victor asked.

Captain Jacob thought the encounter to be humorous but convenient. As the captain boarded the tender to head back to his ship, he remarked, "Don't you two get on one another's nerves now."

Like two stranded souls, Victor and the doctor stood

on the beach and watched the tender ride the waves back to its mothership. They continued watching until the big steamer belched black smoke, turned into the wind, and steamed away. Victor turned to the doctor. "We'd better get up to the house—that wind is enough to cut right through ya."

The doctor responded by pulling his collar snugly around his chin and grabbing his large suitcase.

"I hope you got warmer clothes in that bag," Victor commented, inspecting the doctor from head to toe.

"None adequate for this climate, I'm afraid."

"Here, let me help you," Victor said, slipping his big hand into the handle next to the doctor's.

When the two men entered the little lighthouse living quarters, heat from the woodstove hit them in the face, and the aroma of pea soup filled the warm, cozy room.

"What's the delicious smell?" the doctor asked, flaring his nostrils and sniffing the air like a hound checking for wind scent.

"Split pea soup, been simmering all afternoon—do you like it?"

"Can't recall ever having it," the doctor responded.

Victor pointed to a small door adjacent to the stove. "Put your luggage in there, in Raymond's room. You'll be sleeping there."

"Who is Raymond?" the doctor asked.

"Raymond House—been minding this lighthouse as long as I have. Ray won't mind you using his room. We'll not be seeing him until the weather settles down."

"We are here until he arrives, then?"

"That's right, Doctor. He's my relief."

Doctor Seward gave Victor a quizzical look and entered the small circular bedroom.

Victor fussed over the stove, stoking the fire and making final preparations for supper. He removed two soup bowls from a crude cupboard and placed them on the back of the stove to warm. He ladled hot soup from the boiler and filled each bowl almost to the rim. Then, he retrieved two large pieces of salt meat and placed a piece in each bowl. This was the last of his salt meat, which he used to flavour most cooked meals. Victor always brought extra food to the island—just in case—but he had already gone four extra days and his provisions were seriously diminished. With the weather showing no signs of abating and with an extra mouth to feed, he'd have to get creative.

When Doctor Seward came out of the bedroom, Victor directed him to sit at the table and placed a steaming bowl in front of him. "Here you are, Doctor. Good for what ails ya, as long as you're not offended by a bit of gas later on in the evening," Victor commented mischievously.

"I shall take no offence, old chap. To *fourt* is a sign of good health."

"To do what?" Victor asked, enjoying the lighter tone.

"To *fourt*, man, to *fourt*."

"Oh, to *fart*. Why didn't you say so?" Then, Victor opened the warmer door of the stove, pulled out a china plate full of dumplings, and placed it in the middle of the table. "You can soak the dumplings in your soup or you can save them for afterwards with molasses—that's the way I likes them."

"Can I try them both ways?" asked the doctor.

"Of course. You can have them any way you want. Now, eat up."

And eat up he did, three bowls of soup and the last dumpling smothered in molasses.

"Nothing wrong with your appetite," Victor commented, taking the empty dishes from the table.

"I can hold my own when the food is good, and it was an excellent meal, Victor."

"Nothing fancy, Doctor. Just old-fashioned rough grub."

"Nothing wrong with rough food as long as there's plenty of it."

"Well that's just the point, there's not plenty of it. I'm four days over my three-week shift and the supplies are getting pretty sparse. If this bloody wind doesn't stop, we may be eating a lot of dumplings—without molasses." Victor read a look of concern on the doctor's face and reacted to it. "Not to worry. We won't starve. Tomorrow we'll take the gun and head to the north end of the island, try to shoot a saltwater duck—for a bit of fresh." Victor poured hot water from the kettle into a dishpan. "Do you want to wash or dry?"

"I'm afraid I'm not much of a dishwasher," the doctor responded.

"Well, it's time you learned," Victor remarked, throwing his guest a dish cloth.

"So, where do you hail from, Doctor?" Victor asked.

"You can call me Henry, Victor. I was born, raised, and educated in England. London, to be precise—the mother country." There was pride in his voice.

"You're a long way from home, then. Why did you decide to come here to practice your profession?"

"The need for medical doctors in the overseas colonies is well known among the college of physicians. I felt a calling to do my part, be a humanitarian, I suppose."

"How very noble of you, Henry. God knows we need men like you," Victor commented with a hint of sarcasm.

"And you, Victor, have you ever travelled overseas?"

"Yes, my son, hundreds of time—across the tickle to this island," Victor retorted with a chuckle.

The doctor also chuckled, more out of politeness than from an appreciation of the humour.

By the time the dishes were finished, the light of the day was mostly spent and the room had darkened. Victor reached for the kerosene lamp that was mounted on the wall, lifted the glass chimney, and lit it. Doctor Seward observed every move with interest. "That adds ambience," he commented as a soft light flooded the room.

"It allows us to see how to get about is what it does," Victor countered matter-of-factly.

The doctor threw Victor another quizzical look by furrowing his brow and tilting his head. "Sound Harbour, where I am to set up my practice, does have electric power, doesn't it?"

Victor detected the trepidation and seized the opportunity. "Electric power? No, not this far around the bay. This is not the mother country, Henry."

The doctor's eye's widened and his jaw dropped. "But I was led to believe that ..."

"Can't believe everything you're told," Victor interrupted.

"But how am I to conduct a creditable clinic without electricity?"

"The same way the last doctor did, I s'pose, and all the doctors before him."

"Preposterous!" Doctor Seward exclaimed, throwing his arms into the air.

Victor let out a hearty laugh and slapped the doctor on the back. "Just pullin' your leg, Doc. Of course we have electric power—have had it for nearly 20 years."

"You are very funny, Victor, but I am not laughing!"

"You need to laugh, Henry. Laughter is the best medicine. You're the doctor, you should know that."

A sudden gust of wind hit the lighthouse, causing smoke to baffle down the funnel and puff out around the dampers. "Christ Almighty!" the doctor exclaimed.

Victor ran to the stove and turned a key in the funnel. "Bloody wind is gettin' worse if anything."

Doctor Seward waved his hand in the air like a fan, to clear the lingering smoke. "What do you think, Victor? How long will this storm continue?"

"Difficult to say," Victor responded. "It's been blowing for over a week now. It should soon break. Thing is, we'll need at least a day of civil weather before the sea settles."

"You've been isolated here before, Victor?"

Victor chuckled and responded in a way to indicate that the question was a rhetorical one. "Indeed, I have, many times."

"What is the longest period of time you have been stranded?"

Victor needed no time to contemplate the answer. "It was the year my father died—in February month, it was. They called it the storm of the century, blinding snow, driven by vicious winds. The snow would stop and start, but the wind continued to blow. I was caught out here for nine days with little food and no communication. Poor old father was dead and buried before I got ashore."

"So, you knew nothing of it."

"Oh, I knew, all right."

"How so?"

"I experienced an apparition."

"An apparition? Explain yourself, old chap."

"Well, I had been down to the coal bin and was bringing in a bucket of coal for the night when I saw father's shadow on the staircase leading to the beacon light. I stopped and watched as it descended the spiral stairwell. Then, just before he would have come into view, the shadow disappeared. Father often visited me when I was here, but it was impossible with the storm, so I knew it had to be an apparition. I called out and ascended the stairs, just to satisfy myself, but there was no one there. The strange thing is, I knew that something was wrong, but I wasn't one bit afraid."

"You think I have a leg of rubber that you continue to pull, my friend."

"No, seriously, I saw it as plain as I am seeing you now. I don't know about where you are from, but around here it's common for a recently deceased person to send some kind of a sign to a loved one. Sure, Harrison Reid was fishing on the Labrador coast one summer when his 12-year-old son, Robbie, drowned in Floods Pond while swimming with his friends. Harrison was climbing up the ladder of the schooner's forecastle when someone grabbed his foot. He figured that it was one of the crew members carrying on. But when he looked back, no one was there. Several days later, when the coastal steamer arrived with the mail, Harrison got the news about Robbie: his boy drowned the same day someone grabbed his foot and about the same time. He swears to this day it was Robbie who grabbed him."

"Coincidence, I say. Pure coincidence—and superstition," Doctor Seward insisted, pretending to be uninterested.

"Don't tell that to Raymond," Victor continued. "A few years back, he went to the seal hunt on his off-shift. When he left, his older brother, George, was in bed with what they believed was a bad flu. Sixteen days later they sailed in the harbour with flags flying, indicating a bumper trip. As was the custom, a group had gathered on the wharf to welcome home the sealers. From the deck of the vessel, Raymond scanned the crowd, looking for his family members. His wife, mother, and sister were standing up front, close to the edge of the dock. As he searched farther, he spotted George standing at the very back, with a wool stocking cap pulled over his ears and a scarf around his neck. George must still have that flu, he thought. Then, George turned away and headed up the lane toward his house."

"Don't tell me that George had died," the doctor interjected in a tone of impertinence.

"Indeed, he had," Victor asserted. "When Raymond stepped on the wharf, his mother ran to him and threw her arms around him and told him that poor George had passed away while he was at the ice."

"I'm afraid I shall be unable to sleep tonight, Victor, in fear of being accosted by some manifestation from the other side."

In fact, the doctor did not sleep well that night—not because of Victor's stories, though. It was the wind that kept him awake. It was like nothing he had heard before. It roared constantly, like a powerful locomotive. It howled in the seams around the windows, and it shook the wooden structure with its gusts. The English doctor reasoned that he had arrived at the end of the world, and he questioned his decision to have crossed the Atlantic.

As a result of his restless night, Doctor Seward slept late into the morning. Victor had tended to the beacon light, completed his morning chores, and was preparing a floury mixture to fry up for a late breakfast before the doctor emerged from his room.

"So, how did you sleep, Henry?"

"I'm afraid it did not come easy. I was fearful the building would leave its foundation."

"No worries about that, Doc. Lighthouses are built to stand against the wind—especially this one. Now, grab a plate. Breakfast is ready—nothing fancy, but it'll fill a hole. When we're done, we'll head out to look for something fresh for supper."

The wind was still blowing a gale when the two men left the lighthouse and took to a narrow rock-strewn pathway that meandered around the coastline, dangerously close to the edge of the steep cliffs. The sea crashed against the rocky shoreline, catapulting a foamy spray high into the air. The doctor was dressed in rubber pants and boots belonging to Raymond and Victor's hooded parka. The salty spray settled on his lips and stung his eyes.

At the end of the island, Raymond and Victor had

erected a crude stone shelter to act as a bird blind. The two crawled into it, thankful for the shelter it provided. Victor wedged his gun into a crevice in the rock wall and removed an ammunition bag that he wore over his shoulder. He removed several cartridges and meticulously lined them along a small stone ledge. Then he broke off his shotgun and was about to insert a shell when Doctor Seward spoke. "I have always held a bit of a fascination for guns, Victor. I have read extensively about them, but I have never actually held one. Do you mind if I hold it before you load it?"

"Of course, I don't mind," Victor responded, closing the gun and handing it over.

The doctor took it like one taking a collection plate at a church service. He ran his hand over the polished hardwood stock and along the cold blue metal barrel. He pulled it snug to his shoulder, tilted his head, cocked an eye, and took aim like a child playing with a Christmas present. "This is a breechloader, isn't it?"

"That it is," Victor responded.

"Henry VIII possessed a breechloader, which he also used as a hunting gun to hunt birds. Did you know that, Victor?"

"Can't say I did. What do you think, Doc? Do you like the feel of her?"

"That I do."

"Now, go ahead and cock it."

The doctor placed his delicate hand flat over the hammer and attempted to pull it back, but to no avail.

"No, like this." Victor placed his big thumb on the top of the hammer and pushed down. *Click,* the hammer engaged.

"So, what's the difference between a muzzleloader and a breechloader, Victor?"

"The breechloader is more modern. You break it off and load it at the breech by inserting a cartridge. The muzzleloader is loaded down through the muzzle. You have to pour in loose powder and shot and pack it with a ramrod. Not used anymore. I have one at home, though—belonged to my father."

"Have you shot many birds with this gun, Victor?"

"I've shot my share," Victor responded. Then he began a series of stories about previous hunting adventures, not without some exaggeration. Doctor Seward was the perfect listener. He absorbed every word, interrupting only to encourage additional details. During one of the accounts, the dramatic storyteller suddenly stopped speaking and jerked to attention. Two black ducks were flying straight for the blind. He grabbed the loaded gun, pulled back the hammer and waited. The powder exploded. Doctor

Seward jumped. The two birds tumbled to the ground. The doctor bounced to his feet with excitement. "A bloody fine shot, old chap! You got them both!" he yelled.

"These will give us two good meals," Victor said, picking up the birds. "Here, Doc, you carry the gun."

"Gladly," he replied, taking the gun like one who had been promoted to an upper rank of manhood. Victor began to whistle a tune, and the mood was light as the two hunters made their way back to the lighthouse. Circling one of the deep gulches, Doctor Seward noticed a bird bobbing in the water, close to the rocky shoreline. "There!" he shouted, grabbing Victor's jacket sleeve and pointing.

The bird appeared to have been in some kind of distress and was battering on the water to avoid being washed into the turbulent surf.

"Quick, give me the gun!" Victor demanded, dropping the two birds he was carrying. He strapped the breechloader to his shoulder and began to descend the steep gulch.

"For the love of God, be careful. You'll fall to your death!" the doctor shouted.

Victor continued to inch his way down the steep embankment, carefully testing his foothold with every step. Eventually, he reached a ledge that offered a platform on which to stand, a good gunshot from the water. From this point onward, there was a straight drop into the sea. He quickly loaded the breechloader, carefully took aim, and fired. A splatter of shot pelted the water below, the bird toppled over and floated belly up. Slowly, Victor relaxed his stance, ejected the empty shell, slipped the gun over his shoulder and cautiously retraced his steps. As he neared the rim of the depression, Doctor Seward outstretched his arm; Victor grabbed it and was pulled to solid ground.

"Why did you shoot it, when you knew there was no way to retrieve it?" the doctor asked in a disconcerting tone.

"It was full of oil. Gonna slowly perish. I put it out of its misery," Victor replied.

"How could you tell?"

"I've seen it before."

"Oil? Where did it come from?"

"The big ships purging bilge water. Stuff is full of old base oil. The birds land in it, and it sticks to their feathers, causing them to mat together, losing their usefulness. The birds pick at it, trying to clean themselves, and become poisoned."

"That's horrendous. There should be a law against such a practice," the doctor declared.

"There is," Victor retorted, "but no one seems to give a damn. Come on, let's get home, out of this wind."

Back at the lighthouse, Victor dipped the two birds in a pot of boiling water, and picked and cleaned them. He prepared one for supper and placed it the oven. The other he covered with a dish and placed it in the cold pantry for another time. Again, the doctor ate heartily. "No better a meal could be had in a fine restaurant in London, Victor," the doctor said, pushing back his empty plate and rubbing his belly.

"Would have been better with a bit of salt meat and an extra onion, but not bad, if I have to say so myself," Victor stated with a grin, accepting the compliment.

The doctor did not wait to be asked. "I'll wash," he stated, jumping up the minute Victor poured the dishwater.

After the dishes were cleaned and stored, the lamps lit, and the kindling shaved to start the morning fire, Victor reached into a small cupboard on the wall and removed a well-worn deck of playing cards.

"Do you play cards, Henry?"

"I enjoy a game of bridge and cribbage, but I don't suppose ..."

"One-twenty is the big game around here. It's much better with a crowd, but two can play it. I can teach you if you like."

The doctor learned quickly, and the two played game after game until Victor decided the lamp oil was getting low.

For the next two days the wind continued to assault the island. Each day Victor and the doctor trekked to the bird blind but returned empty-handed. The doctor carried the gun to and from, and, before returning on the second day, Victor encouraged him to fire at a makeshift target. He did so awkwardly and received a firm blow from the gun's recoil. "I think I'll leave the shooting to the expert," he commented.

"Nah, I'll make a hunter out of you yet," Victor teased.

During the evenings, the pair played cards, and a competition developed between them. "Beginners luck," Victor said each time Doctor Seward won a game.

On the morning of the fifth day, Doctor Seward awoke with a jolt. Something was different. There was a stillness—an unnerving silence. No roaring. No howling. No shaking and rattling. There was no wind. The doctor quickly jumped from his bed, dressed, and ran from his room in search of Victor.

The lighthouse keeper was already out and about, fulfilling his duties, when Doctor Seward approached with excitement. "It's civil at last, old chap. Do you think we'll make it to the mainland today?"

Victor stopped what he was doing and looked out over the ocean, toward the horizon. "Depends on when the sea settles down. The wind dropped shortly after midnight, so, maybe later in the day."

Victor was absolutely correct in his prediction. Late in the afternoon he was scanning the tickle through his spyglass when he noticed a small boat heading for the island. "Get your things together, Doc. Raymond is on his way. No time to spare—that wind can come back up as fast as it went down."

The turnaround time was short. A brief report to Raymond, and the doctor and the lighthouse keeper were making their way across the water toward the mainland. As they approached the land, the doctor noticed a small elongated opening in the cliffs that gave passage to the harbour beyond. "Sound Harbour," Victor said, pointing to it.

When they slipped through the narrow gap, Doctor Seward saw, for the first time, the little community that was about to become his home.

The harbour opened into a circular fjord that cut deep into the high cliffs, offering safe haven from the elements. Multicoloured houses dotted the shoreline and were reflected in the still water. Small boats, equally colourful, bobbed on moorings close to the shore. *Pretty,* the doctor thought.

It was almost dark when they docked at the community wharf. A few pre-adolescent boys and a lone adult male in a long black raglan were waiting on the wharf. The adult was Reverend Mercer, there to welcome the new doctor. "Doctor Seward, I presume," he said, extending his hand to the doctor while ignoring Victor. "I was anxious about your whereabouts! It's good to see you. Come, I'll take you to your residence." He turned to one of the boys. "Grab the doctor's bag, lad, and follow along."

The two men, along with all of the boys, headed for the large two-storey doctor's residence located in the middle of the community. Before leaving the wharf, though, Doctor Seward turned back to Victor who was busy securing the boat. "Thank you, Victor, thank you for everything."

Victor responded with a hand salute and a quick nod but did not speak.

Reverend Mercer led the entourage through the narrow road, pointing out various landmarks. When he reached the residence, he dismissed the boys and circled the house to a back porch. He removed a rusty padlock from a freshly painted storm door and ushered the doctor inside, where it was cool and dark. A single light bulb dangled from the middle of the ceiling with a long-beaded chain extending from its porcelain socket. Doctor Seward reached up and pulled the chain. He had to be sure. A dull light flooded the space, and the doctor grinned.

Word of the doctor's arrival spread like news of a broken marriage, and crowds from all along the coast lined up to visit him. Ailments that had gone unattended for weeks needed urgent attention. Small children and pregnant women were his first priority. Doctor Seward quickly realized that his services were in high demand and his job was to be nothing short of challenging.

Nearly three weeks passed before Doctor Seward saw Victor again. It was at the end of an exceptionally busy day, and he was relaxing in his living room with a glass of brandy when a rap came on his front door. Expecting an emergency of some sort, he ditched his brandy and hurried to answer it. Victor was standing there with a large tom turkey tucked underneath his arm. "I was wondering if you'd take a look at my turkey, Doctor. He's got a bad foot—all swollen up—looks like it might be infected."

"Good God, old man, I'm a medical doctor, not a veterinarian," the doctor responded, trying not to appear irritated with the man who had fed, housed, and entertained him.

"Okay, Doctor. I thought I'd check. Sorry to have bothered you," Victor said, turning to leave.

"Victor, stop!" the doctor called. "Bring him around to the back door, I'll take a look at him."

"I don't want to impose, Henry. I understand. It's only a turkey."

"It's okay, Victor, take him around. I'll open the door for you."

The doctor led Victor into a small room at the rear of the house that he used as an examination room. The turkey was placed on a small wooden table and Doctor Seward began to investigate.

"Did you know that Benjamin Franklin wanted to make the turkey, not the Bald Eagle, the national bird of America, Victor?" the doctor asked.

"No," responded Victor. "Did you know that Henry VIII owned a breechloader for hunting birds?"

Both men chuckled.

"There's no doubt it's infected. I'll need to lance it. Do you think you can hold him?"

"I think so," replied Victor, wrapping his strong arms around the frightened bird, and stroking it with his free hand.

"What's his name?" the doctor asked.

"Who?"

"The turkey."

"He doesn't have a name."

"Well, then, I shall name him Oedipus."

"Odd name. Where does it come from?"

"It's from ancient Greek mythology, from a play by Sophocles, about the king of Thebes who killed his father and married his mother."

"Married his mother?" Victor was repulsed. "Harrison Boland from down the bay married his first cousin. I thought that was bad enough."

"Well, he didn't know it was his mother. He was abandoned by his parents as an infant. His father bound his feet together with a pin and left him on a mountaintop. A shepherd found him and, because his feet were swollen, he called him Oedipus—Oedipus means swollen feet in the Greek language."

"Well then, Oedipus is as good a name as any, I s'pose," Victor concurred.

"Hold him firm now," the doctor commanded as he drew a scalpel across the large inflamed abscess. Yellow pus drained from the incision. The doctor massaged the area to extract the infectious fluid and cleansed it with an antiseptic solution. "There that should be good," he concluded.

"Are you going to bandage it?"

"No point, he'd only pick it off. Besides, it needs to drain. Here, I'll give you this antibiotic cream. Give the wound an ample coating once a day for the next week or so."

"Mary will have to do that, then. I'm back on the island tomorrow for another three weeks. By the way, Doc," Victor said, tucking Oedipus under his arm, "when I finish this shift, we'll be starting up our Christmas card games of One-twenty. Would you like to join us?"

"I think I'd like that, Victor. Thank you for asking."

"Very good, then. I'll send you word when I finish my shift."

The card game was the last Saturday before Christmas Day, 8 p.m., at Victor's house. Mary, Victor's wife, met the doctor at the door when he arrived. It was the first time he had met her. *A lovely lady*. The other men were already there: Victor's two brothers, Jack and Joe; Tommy Sweetland; and Tacker Duffett. The doctor made the sixth hand. He was quickly taught how to play the game with more than two players and, for two hours, the men thumped their fists hard on the table every time a trick was won or a cross-play made. There was little time for conversation, only the intensity of the game. Victor was hosting, so it was his responsibility to provide the prize. It was a hen that he had butchered earlier that day. It was picked and cleaned and ready to be presented to the lucky winner. As fate should have it, Victor accumulated the most points and won his own bird.

As the doctor was making ready to leave after the game, Mary emerged from the upstairs and addressed him. "How did you enjoy the card game, Doctor?" she inquired.

"Just lovely, Mary, thank you very much. A little more challenging with six players as opposed to two, but I think I held my own."

"What about Christmas Day, Doctor? Do you have any plans?"

"No plans, Mary. I am hoping it to be a peaceful day at home with everyone staying healthy and no calls."

"It's settled, then, you will be having Christmas dinner with us. There's only me and Victor, so we'd love to have you."

"In that case, Mary, I graciously accept your offer."

Doctor Seward awoke on Christmas morning to a fresh blanket of snow and the sound of the church bell. He felt lonely for his family, and he missed the streets of London at this time of the year—the decorations, the people, the sounds, and the smells. He was happy that he was going to Victor and Mary's for dinner.

Doctor Seward was not a religious man, but he decided

to attend the Christmas morning church service, as he had always done at home. He had not gone to church since arriving in Sound Harbour. Reverend Mercer was noticeably happy to see him and acknowledged his presence, causing the doctor some embarrassment. He had never enjoyed being the centre of attention.

After the church service the doctor went directly to Victor's house. When he opened the door, the mouth-watering smell of Christmas dinner met him in the porch. *These people are good cooks.*

Victor greeted his guest with a warm handshake. "Merry Christmas, Henry, come on in and we'll have a little Christmas toddy before our dinner."

"I didn't think you drank alcohol, Victor," the doctor commented.

"Only at Christmas time, Doc, only at Christmas." Then, Victor pulled a bottle of dark navy rum from a small corner cupboard.

As he was pouring the drinks, Mary entered the room carrying a small package wrapped in silver Christmas paper. "Here you are, Doctor. 'Tis not much, but a little something in the spirit of the season."

The doctor was touched. "I'm afraid I don't have a present for you," he stated apologetically.

"Don't be so silly, Doctor. Sure, 'tis nothing we need. Your company is gift enough for us. Now, go on, open it."

"Woollen stockings and mittens. How thoughtful, Mary. Knit by you, no doubt?"

"Of course. I was going to do a cap to match the mitts but ran short on wool. You'll get it later."

"I need to check the bird," Victor voiced, gulping down the last of his rum. He crossed the floor to the stove, pulled open the oven door, withdrew a large roaster and removed its cover. A tantalizing smell filled the doctor's nostrils. "Take a look at this, Doc," he said with pride, slightly tipping the roaster toward the doctor, revealing a large turkey, browned to perfection. Caramelized onions floated in a succulent-looking broth.

The doctor looked from the turkey to Victor and back again to the turkey. "Oedipus?" he asked.

"I'm afraid so," Victor responded.

The doctor was not deterred, though, nor was his appetite affected. He ate until his belly hurt.

"Nothing wrong with your appetite, Doctor," Mary remarked.

"So Victor has told me."

It was the first of many meals Doctor Seward was to have at Victor and Mary's house—especially when the yield of a successful hunting trip was on the menu. Victor frequently invited the doctor on bird-hunting trips, and the busy doctor took full advantage whenever he could free himself. The shooting was always left to Victor, but Doctor Seward enjoyed the outings immensely.

As the years passed, the doctor needed no invitation to visit his two friends. He'd simply drop in whenever he needed some friendly company or felt the urge for a home-cooked meal.

Doctor Seward also became a regular on the card-game circuit and often hosted the game at the doctor's residence. Slowly, he worked his way into the fabric of rural living and learned the ins and outs of outport doctoring.

The year of the flu epidemic was a particular challenging one. Doctor Seward ran himself ragged tending to sick patients all along the coast. The very young and the elderly were especially vulnerable, with several deaths, including three right in Sound Harbour. He too became infected but forced himself from his sickbed to tend to his patients. During this busy and demanding time, there was no contact with Victor and Mary. Then, one day, Victor showed up at his clinic—without a turkey under his arm.

"I had to come to see you, Doctor. This bloody flu has been lingering half the winter and got me knocked for a loop."

The doctor questioned his friend and conducted a thorough examination. Victor's symptoms were not characteristic of influenza nor were they common to those presented by other patients. This caused the doctor some worry, but he kept his concerns to himself.

After the flu epidemic ran its natural course and Victor did not improve—in fact, worsened—Doctor Seward realized that Victor needed special tests that were available only in the city. He wired off referrals to the General Hospital with specific instructions. After what seemed like an eternity, his request was finally honoured, and a very reluctant Victor boarded the coastal steamer on his way to be prodded and probed for days on end.

While Victor was away, Tommy Sweetland hosted the first card game of the season with Herman Baker sitting in for Victor. Doctor Seward won the prize that night: a hamper of fresh vegetables. This, though, did not offset the fact that Victor was missing—the game was not the same without his friend. The next week Tacker Duffett hosted the game. Doctor Seward came up with a feeble excuse why he could not attend.

Victor returned looking more like one who had been to a prison camp than a hospital. He delivered to the doctor a large sealed envelope from the General Hospital with the word *Confidential* stamped across it. Doctor Seward knew this was Victor's report, and he opened it apprehensively. His suspicions had been correct all along. The tumour was malignant, and inoperable. Nothing could be done. There was to be no more bird-hunting trips, no more card games, no more mouth-watering dinners.

Doctor Seward visited his friend as frequently as he could and observed the once-capable, able-bodied man deteriorate to a mere caricature of his formal self. With each visit he felt more and more helpless. All he could do was administer pain medication and offer moral support. When Victor weakened to the point of being incapacitated, Mary set up a bed in the parlour so that she did not have to continuously climb up and down the stairs to tend to him.

On one visit, Mary followed the doctor into the porch as he left. She reached into the boot closet behind the door and withdrew an elongated object wrapped in an old blanket. "Here you are, Doctor. Victor wanted me to give you this."

The instant the doctor gripped the blanket he knew that the enfolded item was Victor's breechloader. "Mary, I cannot accept Victor's gun."

"Nonsense! He'll not be needing it anymore. There's no one in this world he'd rather have it than you. He made me promise ..." Mary objected, her eyes becoming misty and her voice cracking. The doctor accepted the gift without speaking, because a lump had risen in his throat.

When he got home, he unwrapped Victor's prized breechloader gun and caressed it the way he had in the bird blind on the northern end of Green Island. He remembered the initial meeting with Victor and the days spent in the lighthouse with him. He recalled the many card games, and he thought about Oedipus. He wondered what happened to Henry VIII's breechloader. *In a museum somewhere, no doubt.* He knew exactly where Victor's gun was going.

Doctor Seward rummaged around the storage room of the doctor's residence, located two screw hooks, and strategically fixed them to the far wall of his bedroom. There, he mounted Victor's gun, on a slight angle, pointing skyward.

On the next visit to Victor's house, it was obvious that his friend was in discomfort. His muscles twitched, his eyes were recessed, and his face was contorted. As the doctor administered pain medication, the frail man reached up and grasped the doctor's arm. "You know what I am,

Henry," he murmured in a feeble voice, his breathing laboured. "I'm a bird ... a bird full of oil." His gaze met the doctor's. It was sustained and penetrating. His grip tightened, his bony fingers bit into the doctor's skin. Neither man spoke further but their communication was understood. Doctor Seward knew exactly what his friend was asking of him.

That evening Victor's words played heavy on the doctor's mind. His medical training had taught him to protect and to value life, but now he pondered how quality fit into this equation. Over the years he had come to realize the virtue of life but, at the same time, he understood its fragility. He evaluated the spiritual against the scientific. He cursed the iniquitousness of being, and he assessed his own existence. In the end, he unlocked his medicine cabinet, retrieved a vial of morphine and placed it in his doctor's kit.

In the morning Doctor Seward made the familiar but now dreaded trek to Victor's house. Mary was sitting at the table drinking tea and eating bread that had been toasted over the hot coals of the woodstove. "Have a cup of tea, Doctor," she invited.

"Yes, thank you, Mary. I think I will." The doctor accepted, wanting to stall the unimaginable task he had planned.

Together, the two sat at the kitchen table and talked for a long time. Mary reminisced about the past, when she and Victor were young, dating, and madly in love. She was philosophical and wondered how she would react when the time came, how she would cope on her own. She wondered what life was all about. Doctor Seward listened, interjecting only to offer comfort.

Eventually, he excused himself and went into the parlour, where Victor was sleeping. He did not wake him. Methodically, he opened his kit, removed the vial of morphine, drew 120 milligrams (a dosage large enough to induce perpetual sleep) into a syringe, and located a vein. He queried the necessity to sterilize the entry site. But he followed protocol, applied alcohol, and, with a shaking hand, positioned the tip of the needle. He placed his thumb on the plunger, but, before making the injection, he stopped, stood up, and wiped his brow with the sleeve of his jacket. He rushed to the kitchen, removed the damper from the woodstove, and squirted the contents of the syringe into the fire. The fire hissed momentarily, but soon puffed and again glowed vibrantly.

That night, sleep did not come easy for the doctor. A dense fog had descended upon the land, bringing with it a deafening stillness. Every creak and groan of the old house was audible. Each stimulated memories and evoked feelings, causing the distraught doctor to lie awake, twisting and turning. Sometime, well after the midnight hour, a distinct click jolted him upright in his bed. It was a noise he had heard a hundred times before. It was the sound of Victor's gun being cocked. The doctor reached for the chain hanging from the light bulb above his bed and pulled it. Warily, he got out of bed and crossed the cold floor to where Victor's gun was hanging on the wall. He was not afraid. He looked up expecting to see the hammer of the breechloader in an engaged position. It was not. The drone of the foghorn sneaked into the room like an unwelcome visitor and Doctor Seaward sighed heavily. He knew that his friend was gone, but he was not sad—sadness had left him. Instead, he thought about his family back in the old country. The foghorn droned again and Dr. Seaward knew that he would be going home to stay.

The Old Man

I saw an old man staring into the sea.
I saw the old man, and the old man, he saw me.
His shoulders were rounded; his whiskers were white.
His face was wrinkled, but his eyes, they were bright.

The sea, it was quicksilver, shiny as glass.
A crystal reflection into this old man's past.
Little boats were fishing, the nets were all full.
Seagulls were screaming, *heave, haul,* and *pull.*

A little town nestled in a now empty cove.
A church bell ringing from the cliffs up above.
People were smiling and scurrying about.
Times were hard but no one went without.

The children were playing upon a stagehead.
Catching crafty conners, with nothing to dread.
There was Jackie and Joe, Emma, and the twin.
Two were his own, and the others were his kin.

Friends came calling when day's work was done,
Card games and music and old-fashioned fun.
When an angry sea claimed three of their own,
All grieved together with no one left alone.

The smell of romance sweetened the salty air.
A girl in a bandana was standing there.
Smiles of contentment upon her pretty face,
She said I love you, and I love this little place.

She was his shipmate, through his journey of life.
A stoic woman, a mother and his wife.
Life altered course on the day that she died,
His aged heart shattered and his bright eyes cried.

I saw an old man staring into the sea.
I knew the old man, 'cause the old man, he is me.

About the Author

Bruce Stagg grew up in the 1950s and 1960s in Catalina, a rural fishing community on Newfoundland's east coast. This time and place are the source of inspiration for the stories in this book. A retired educator, Bruce began his writing career by creating plays for his students. He has since published a book of plays, two books of short stories, a children's book, and two collections of creative nonfiction. He has also written and produced a number of other plays.

Bruce currently lives in Hillview, Trinity Bay, with his wife, Dale. He enjoys rural living, travelling, and spending time with his four grandchildren—but he always finds time to write.